Praise for *Homef*

T0246690

"If you've given up on the power of the sh~~o~~.. ~~story, this book~~ will change your mind for good. In *Homefront*, Kelly gives us characters tied together by a proximity to war, but it's truly America's story, in the hands of a master of the genre."

—Karin Tanabe, author of *The Sunset Crowd*

"Victoria Kelly leverages her skills as a writer with her own experiences as a fighter pilot's spouse to capture military life from fourteen unique and engaging perspectives. *Homefront* is beautiful, heartbreaking, and unflinchingly honest."

—Ward Carroll, author of *Punk's War,* YouTuber, and retired naval aviator

"Victoria Kelly has penned gorgeous short stories in *Homefront* that encompass the deep nuances within families affiliated with the military. Written tenderly and respectfully, each thought-provoking story is a page-turner and a new experience, allowing me to take a breath and dive into the intricacies and important daily lives of her characters."

—Tif Marcelo, *USA Today* bestselling author of *In a Book Club Far Away*

"In a market overwhelmed by male voices and perspectives, *Homefront* adds important diversity to the literary landscape and does so in a powerful way. Kelly's writing is exceptional, the characters are interesting, the writing about military culture is convincing, and the storylines are thoughtful and well-paced. Every aspect of *Homefront* is authentic."

—Caleb Cage, U.S. Army veteran, author of
Desert Mementos: Stories of Iraq and Nevada

"The stories that comprise *Homefront* wrestle with classic dilemmas of desire and regret, hope and loss, in new and often wrenching ways. In this superb, eminently readable collection, Victoria Kelly cements herself as one of our great chroniclers of the war and peace found in contemporary American life."

—Matt Gallagher, author of *Daybreak* and *Youngblood*

THE BATTLE BORN SERIES

Caleb S. Cage, *Series Editor*

From 1864, when it joined the United States at the height of the Civil War, Nevada has played an important role in the nation's wars, the training of its soldiers, and the development of its military technologies. The books in this series explore the lives, families, and literature of the soldiers who have served the state and the nation. Series editor Caleb Cage invites fiction, creative nonfiction, and scholarly works from any geographic area that engage with the issues at the heart of the American military.

Gunning for Ho: Vietnam Stories
H. Lee Barnes

Acceleration Hours: Stories
Jesse Goolsby

Desert Mementos: Stories of Iraq and Nevada
Caleb S. Cage

Minimal Damage: Stories of Veterans
H. Lee Barnes

Remembering Korea: A Boy Soldier's Story
H. K. Shin

American Commander in Spain: Robert Hale Merriman
and the Abraham Lincoln Brigade
Marion Merriman and Warren Lerude

A Private War: An American Code Officer in the Belgian Congo
Robert Laxalt

Homefront: Stories
Victoria Kelly

Homefront

Stories

VICTORIA KELLY

UNIVERSITY OF NEVADA PRESS | *Reno & Las Vegas*

University of Nevada Press | Reno, Nevada 89557 USA
www.unpress.nevada.edu
Copyright © 2024 by University of Nevada Press
All rights reserved
Manufactured in the United States of America

FIRST PRINTING

Cover design by TG Design
Cover photography: Shutterstock.com by Kim Ruoff; Maxy M; Kryuchka Yaroslav; and
aspen rock.

LIBRARY OF CONGRESS CATALOGING-IN-PUBLICATION DATA ON FILE
ISBN 978-1-64779-144-5 (paper)
ISBN 978-1-64779-145-2 (ebook)
LCCN 2023942820

For Nate–

I wish I knew you then.

And for Alida, Rose, Everly, Lexi, and Carter—

No matter how old you get,

you can always come home.

Contents

Contents

A Note from the Author

I wrote these stories over ten years when I was the wife of a fighter pilot, during his three wartime deployments to Iraq and Afghanistan. During the first deployment, my greatest challenge was the loneliness of being a newlywed alone in a new city. By the third, I was the mother of two toddlers, living in a hotel room after my house was flooded by a hurricane. I grew up a whole lot.

These fourteen stories follow women whose lives have been impacted by war and military service in direct and indirect ways—from a Navy wife who discovers that her neighbor is having an affair while their husbands are deployed to a student who makes an unexpected connection with a German concentration camp survivor. The themes of loneliness, identity, guilt, and love were all emotions I grappled with during that time.

From the outside, I might have seemed like the "perfect" military wife. But nothing's ever what it seems. War, from the time of Odysseus and Penelope, has always taken its toll on families. My grandfather was a medic in Nagasaki after the atomic bomb fell. I never met him; he turned to alcohol to cope with what he'd been through and died in his forties. My own first marriage eventually ended in divorce.

When I started this book, I was a new wife, living near the naval base in Meridian, Mississippi. I had just graduated from the Iowa Writers' Workshop. I finished the stories four cities and too many homes later to count. Still, that old military life—the good and the bad—echoes through the years. My oldest daughters' father, remarried now, just finished a year-long deployment to Africa. I also married again, to a former Marine sniper platoon commander who fought in Ramadi during some of the most dangerous conflicts of the Iraq War. I've learned that no matter what role you played—pilot, soldier, officer, mother, spouse—you never really leave that life behind.

These stories and the people in them are fictional, but they wouldn't exist without the many real experiences that shaped them. They were some of the most meaningful adventures of my life.

HOMEFRONT

Finding the Good Light

Diane was twenty-seven when she was cast in her first movie, an age considered old in the film industry. And she felt it; in the years before that, she had already lived a whole life, and so had her cast mates, most of whom were even older than she was. Some nights while they were filming, they sat around in one of the tiny trailers, drinking from plastic cups of beer and wondering how it was they'd all ended up in the backwaters of Floribama, trying to be movie stars.

The film was about the Depression years when Claudette Colbert made *It Happened One Night* with Clark Gable, and Diane was cast as Claudette. It was a tiny movie from a tiny studio based forty-five minutes outside of Hollywood, and there was a lightheartedness among the cast, an unspoken acknowledgment that they were never going to be able to pull off such a show believably, so why even worry about it?—they were, after all, unknown actors playing famous actors playing characters from one of the most famous movies of the prewar years. Bill, who played Clark Gable, was a veterinarian from Philadelphia, and Vincent, who was cast as Paramount director Frank Capra, had come straight from the community theater of White Plains, New York. All of them had been discovered in one way or another by Romey Layfield, the director, who said their never having been on-screen before would help people "suspend their disbelief."

For budget reasons, the whole thing was filmed in Alabama over the course of one hot, dusty summer, so by the time the movie premiered in nine theaters, and then nine hundred, and then—to everyone's amazement—nine thousand, Diane had only been to California one time, to sign her contract before the whole thing began.

She didn't have an agent or a résumé longer than one line, and she hadn't been able to get another acting job after the filming ended, before the movie came out and people learned her name. But then, suddenly, they were calling her—wealthy, important people from Los Angeles and New York, journalists and clothing designers and theater directors who had turned her down for half a dozen roles in the weeks before. She was offered ten jobs in the period of two days, and she didn't know who to say yes to, so she jotted down the directors' names on a yellow legal pad by the phone and said she would call them back.

The first time she was followed by a photographer, it was right after *The Girl from Saint-Mandé* was picked up by Regal Theaters, and she was living in a tiny apartment across from a church in Morristown, New Jersey, where she'd grown up. Her parents were long dead by then, and the aunt who'd raised her had moved to Naples, Florida, but she still felt a strange attachment to that New Jersey town—its parks and *panederías* and even the luxury condominium building that had replaced Epstein's department store. And she liked the heavy, solid permanence of the gray stone church across the street, which always had a candle lit near the altar.

It happened while she was in the parking garage of Century 21, on her way home from buying a dress for a friend's party. It was late, after the store had closed, and she had emerged alone into the dark garage when she thought she heard something behind her in the stairwell. It was starting to be the time of night when people didn't go out in certain neighborhoods in Morristown, and she was frightened when the man, tall and dressed entirely in black, appeared behind her. She was sure he was going to mug or rape her. But then, instead of attacking her, he pulled out a camera and took her picture, and the shot—her stricken, doe-eyed expression of terror—appeared the following week in *Life & Style*. She took the magazine into the supermarket bathroom and studied the photograph. It would have been thrilling if it had been any other picture. But it was strange, and almost worrisome—how stunningly, trustingly childlike she appeared. And she realized that this was what people saw when they looked at her—someone who hadn't yet been tainted by the drama of drugs or money or sex, someone whose best years weren't already behind her. This was why they loved her.

◆ ◆ ◆

It was only a matter of time, of course, before the truth got out—that she had already been married and divorced; that she'd been to eight funerals—*eight*—of women whose husbands had died in various explosions on the ground or in the air over Iraq; that her parents had been vacationing in Mexico City during the earthquake of 1985, when she was just a year old, and never made it back.

She met Jack when she was nineteen, just out of high school and on a trip to Pensacola to look at condominiums with her aunt. Jack was twenty-two and in the first weeks of flight school. The war in Iraq had just started, and he was so full of energy, so swollen with life that she almost believed he could give her back all those years she'd lost after her parents died. In the Navy, even officers married young, and within four months they were dancing their first wedding dance on a beach outside the base, celebrating with her aunt and Jack's mother and father and a handful of his flight school classmates.

She remembered to show her pink ID card in the commissary before the cashier had to ask for it, figured out how to budget on Jack's ensign's salary, and learned to lie and say she wasn't a military wife on her job applications so they wouldn't know she'd probably be gone in another year. Most important, she settled easily into the wives' groups. She liked the other women; most of them were bored like her, and they called one another a lot, mostly for no reason, and went to movies and played tennis at the courts on base on the weekends.

After three years and four moves, Jack had his wings and was flying over Baghdad. They began talking about children when he got back. But almost as soon as he was home, he was gone again, to Key West for the next round of workups, and then he went back over the ocean, this time to Afghanistan. She read about SAM sites in the news and every night while he was gone, when she came home from her job selling dresses in a bridal salon, she always expected to see the chaplain and the other wives standing on her doorstep. Midway through, she got the call that it had happened after all, but to someone else's husband, and a few hours later she found herself in the sad huddle on some other woman's driveway. Nothing was the same after that.

One miscarriage, two deployments, and seven years after their wedding day, her husband came home from Afghanistan to tell her on the tarmac, full of remorse, that he'd met someone else on the aircraft carrier, a female flight officer just out of the Academy, and he didn't want to be married anymore, not to her at least.

She had been an officer's wife, had gone to parties with admirals. But standing alone in the foyer of their house after he had gone, she understood with sudden clarity that all she really had was a high school education and a string of retail jobs on her résumé.

◆ ◆ ◆

Romey found her sitting at a Waffle House midway between Virginia Beach and Naples. When he told her he was casting for a movie, she tried not to look him in the face. "I don't think I'm the person you're looking for," she said, sliding a little closer to the outside edge of her booth in case he tried to sit down next to her. She'd heard about men like him.

"Yes," he insisted. "You're exactly it." He seemed nervous and excited, and she asked him what he was doing at a Waffle House in South Carolina if he really was a Hollywood director.

"I'm visiting my son," he said. "He lives here."

"I'm actually on my way to Florida," she told him, wishing he would leave. "And I'm not an actress. I'm sorry."

He waved his hand. "It doesn't matter if you don't know how to act. I can't pay you very much anyway." He caught himself. "But I *will* pay you," he added.

"Pay me for what, exactly?" she wanted to ask.

But he didn't seem like he was after sex. He was around the age her father would have been if he had lived, and he stood there in front of her table with his shoulders slightly hunched, as if he was trying not to take up too much space. When she noticed he was wearing sneakers with white gym socks and pants that stopped at his ankles, the way she knew her father would have dressed if he had aged past thirty-two, she felt a warm, complete swelling of affection toward him, like the air expanding inside a balloon.

A few hours later, she met him in his hotel room to "talk about the script." She was still dubious about his intentions, but he didn't try to hit on her, and he really did have a script laid out on the wooden coffee table.

"Claudette Colbert," he said. Diane hadn't heard of her, but he showed her a picture, and she looked up at him in disbelief. She really did look like Claudette Colbert. Why had no one told her before? She had never really thought of herself as beautiful, but here was this woman who had been famous, and people had *loved* this woman, and this woman *looked like her*. And she thought, giddy, I'm going to be in a movie.

Two weeks later the divorce papers had been filed and she was driving out to California to go over the contract.

◆ ◆ ◆

In the end, instead of signing with one of the big studios after she became famous, she agreed to do another of Romey's films. There wasn't a question of anything else, really. He had saved her, and not in the way Jack had saved her. He was just honest with her from the start: that he wasn't famous, and she probably wouldn't ever be famous either, and neither would Bill or Vincent or the rest of the cast. They were all just trying to be a part of something they could look back on and say, I did that, I was there.

But by the time she signed with Romey for the second film there were rumors that *The Girl from Saint-Mandé* would be nominated for the SAG awards, she had appeared twenty-two times in the supermarket tabloids, and she was being regularly followed by photographers. They went through her trash and published a list of which junk foods and which health foods she ate, which birth control pills she was using, and how she was paying only $700 a month for a studio apartment in the rundown Latino section of Morristown, New Jersey, when there were a dozen new yuppie townhomes four blocks away. They loved her for being "down to earth." Her aunt called from Florida and said all the ladies kept asking her why Diane didn't have an agent yet, and why she hadn't done any commercials or signed any endorsement deals, and why she hadn't moved to California or New York. "You shouldn't stay in that apartment. We're worried about you. It's not safe in that neighborhood."

"I like living outside the city," Diane said. "I can go in on the train when I need to audition, but it's not so crazy out here."

"Do you have two locks?"

"Yes," she lied. "I have three."

What nobody realized was that she was still trying to live on the $15,000 she'd gotten from the divorce and the little bit of money she'd made from *The Girl from Saint-Mandé,* because Romey's new project wouldn't start filming until the spring. No one knew that she spent her days running the lines over and over again in front of the mirror, or that she didn't take any calls about commercials because she was terrified that the other directors would discover the truth—that she'd fooled them all, that she wasn't really an actress after all, just some girl from New Jersey who'd happened to be sitting in a Waffle House at just the right time.

Romey's second movie was being filmed in New York. A love story about a young woman who had inherited a "doll hospital" in Greenwich Village, it was an exploration of the loss of simpler, better times. The budget for the film was much larger than the last one; the city closed down the street for filming, and Romey found her a room in the Washington Square Hotel. He and his wife, Barbara, were staying in the room next door, and the first night Barbara came over with Chinese food. Diane found herself telling her all about the divorce and how Jack had called to congratulate her after seeing the movie, but she really couldn't figure out whether he was apologizing for leaving her or congratulating himself for her fame, and how all the smug glory of that moment she'd been anticipating was lost in her confusion.

"Honey," Barbara said, fluffing her faded blond hair, "you're a *star* now. You understand that, don't you?"

Diane smiled. "I've only been in one movie."

Barbara touched her arm gently. "What I mean is, who gives a *shit* what that idiot boy said? And what are you doing out there in New Jersey? You've got to get on with it. Move into the city. Do another movie if you need more money. Do a TV show. Get a boyfriend. Do something."

"I'm doing this movie."

Barbara frowned. "You should go meet up with some of the other girls tonight. It'd be good for you." She stood up abruptly and left the room. Diane stared after her, blinking back tears, until Barbara burst back a few minutes later with a pile of dresses over her arm.

Then Diane tried not to cry for real, because it was something a mother would do, pretending to be mad but really loving you.

Two hours later, Diane was tottering down Bleeker Street in Christian Louboutins and a sequined dress, trying to find the club one of the other actresses had mentioned. Rachel, who Diane thought was unquestionably more famous than her, was playing her sister in the movie, and had been in dozens of movies Diane had seen over the years. But although she had been friendly, Diane couldn't possibly imagine becoming friends with her or any of the other girls, couldn't possibly imagine thinking of herself as one of them.

She was peering up at the numbers on the buildings when she was spotted, first by one photographer and then by six more, who were staking out the neighborhood where the movie was being filmed. She rarely went out at night, and she was immediately blinded by the glittering whiteness of the flashbulbs. She didn't want to be one of those celebrities who covered their faces, pretending to be annoyed, but she didn't want to make a show of the situation either, so she waved, a little awkwardly, and continued looking up at the building numbers. She could feel herself shivering in the sleeveless dress, and her posture was always terrible when she was cold. She wondered whether they would have recognized her if she'd been wearing jeans.

"Diane!" They pressed in on her. They were all men in their mid-thirties, and they were all wearing similar dark jeans and gray T-shirts. "Do you have a date tonight? Are you moving to New York? What's it like working with Romey again?" Some of them shouted their questions with smirks on their faces, and she couldn't tell if they were mocking her or whether that was just how it seemed to her. She had the paralyzing suspicion that they didn't think of her as a real actress at all.

They pushed closer and she shook her head, but they kept snapping their flashbulbs, and she couldn't understand why they would want dozens of pictures of her doing the same thing, walking down a street by herself at night. She was only a little afraid. Mostly she felt a fleeting sense of elation, quickly overcome by a terrible loneliness.

"Diane!" She heard a woman's voice calling to her from across the street, and looked over to see Rachel standing on the sidewalk, stamping out a cigarette. "We're over here!"

The photographers turned too at the sound of Rachel's voice. Rachel had dyed her hair cotton-candy pink for the movie, and Diane wondered how they could have missed her before; she seemed to have mastered, over the years, the art of disappearing in the most obvious of places, of being just enough like other girls to blend in, but somehow apart from them too, somehow better.

Diane darted across the street, nearly tripping in her heels. The photographers crowded behind her, but Rachel pulled her quickly inside the club doors. "You came! We didn't know if you would." Her breath smelled of cigarettes and mojito mint. "Well, *I* thought you would, but Jessica said she didn't think so."

Diane looked up as a crescendo of piano music came floating in from the other room. They weren't in a club as she had thought, but standing in the lobby of what appeared to be an old theater. "What is this place?"

"Oh, it's *wonderful*." Rachel lowered her voice. "It's a *strip club*." Diane pulled back, and Rachel laughed. "You should see your face right now. I'm kidding." She grinned. "It's cabaret." She enunciated the syllables as if they were three complete words, *cab-ar-et*.

Diane laughed too, pretending to be relieved, although she couldn't remember quite what the difference was between a strip club and a cabaret.

"Jessica found it. You should see some of these girls. They're seriously talented." Rachel pulled out another cigarette and sucked on it without lighting it. "Anyway, it's so much better than Tenjune, all those sweaty guys and those chicks with their cell phone cameras following you into the bathroom."

Diane realized that Rachel's new cigarette was fake, one of those plastic menthol devices, and she was surprised. There was a kind of vulnerability to it that made Rachel seem like an ordinary woman, someone who was trying to become a better version of herself.

Rachel led Diane into the main area of the theater, where the rows of cushioned seats had been removed to make room for two dozen tiny cocktail tables and chairs. Jessica waved them over to a table in the middle of the room. She turned to a man and woman seated beside her, introducing them as Marlena and David, a couple in their thirties she and Rachel had only just met. They seemed to have no idea who the three girls were, even Rachel with her candy-pink hair. "They've been in St. Petersburg the past two years," Jessica said. "David was in graduate school there. He's writing a *book*."

Diane glanced around the room. No one else seemed to have noticed them either. On the stage, a half dozen girls in beaded headdresses and thigh-high dresses strutted to the Dean Martin song "Ain't That a Kick in the Head." One of the girls actually appeared to be singing the song herself, not using a guide track. When the girls peeled off their dresses to reveal black ribbon-and-lace corsets, the audience cheered. Rachel and Jessica clapped loudly, and Diane found herself clapping too, drawn into this seductive, glittering underworld where they could all watch someone else for a change.

They ordered drinks and Diane marveled at how strange it felt to be sitting in a roomful of people after months of hermitage in her Morristown studio.

There had been a photographer who'd surprised her once as she was coming out of a ladies' room in a bus station after visiting her aunt. He'd leaned in to take her picture but then, abruptly, frowned and put the camera down. When she asked him why he'd stopped, he said in a thick French accent, "For a lot of people, you know, it makes them happy. To be noticed."

She gawked at him. "How do you know it doesn't make me happy?"

He shrugged, and she was annoyed. "What if it did? Make me happy, I mean."

"Then," he said, "I would take your picture."

He was only a little older than her, handsome in a beatnik way, and for a moment she had a vision of the two of them, this photographer and her, sitting on a secondhand couch together in some townhouse in Brooklyn, watching a movie. But before she could say anything he had moved back into the crowd and was gone, and she wondered, for a long time after that, whether he had even been real, or whether he was someone her dead parents had sent, perhaps, to watch out for her.

When the waitress brought her a vodka tonic ("It won't stain your teeth," Barbara had told her, "or make you fat"), and a trio of new dancers came onstage, she felt her head getting lighter. She leaned back in her chair and watched the dancers sweep in and out of the lights. They wore pouts painted on with red lipstick, and thick, black eyeliner winged out from the corners of their eyes. They seemed to have come striding straight out from another era, when it was sexier to stop at a bra and panties than to go all the way.

Diane's best friend in high school was a Mormon named Levi who ended up moving to Chile after graduation for his two-year mission and then staying there. In the four years she had known him he had never once tried to kiss her, and he had averted his eyes when she changed in front of him, something she had done in part to prompt him to look at her. She felt he saw her as inadequate somehow, tainted or misguided by her Catholic faith, and even though she hadn't seen him in years she wondered what he would make of her divorce and her upcoming sex scene in the movie, which she dreaded.

"My little fallen sparrow," she imagined him saying from his rented room in Valparaiso, reaching across the continents to touch her cheek.

Onstage, the trio had started dancing to a song by the Andrews Sisters, singing it seductively slower than the original. Jessica prodded Diane in the side. "All these girls are crazy good, right? Come backstage with us. Rachel wants to talk to them about the movie. She thinks she could get some of them parts as extras."

Diane slid out of her chair, following Rachel through the maze of tables. They were all a little drunk on cocktails, and Jessica tripped in the side lobby, clutching at Diane's arm and dragging her down also. They fell in a heap on the red-carpeted floor, coughing with laughter, and Rachel's menthol cigarette fell out of her pocket when she reached down to help them up, prompting even more laughter, until one of the dancers came out from backstage to ask them to be quiet.

"Holy *shit*," the girl said, recognizing the three of them lying in a tumble on the floor. "You're—God, I'm so sorry, I didn't know."

Rachel jumped up and grasped both the girl's hands in hers. "You're so *good*. We *loved* you."

The girl gaped at her. She was younger in person than she had appeared onstage; she couldn't have been more than nineteen. With her makeup scrubbed off she had a face strangely like Diane's: the same round features and tiny nose. Diane felt like she was looking at a younger, cleaner version of herself.

"But what are you doing *here*?" the girl asked them.

Rachel laughed. "More like what are *you* doing here? You have an amazing voice."

The dancer blushed. "You can come see backstage if you want."

The dressing room wasn't much bigger than a closet. The dancers were huddled five to a mirror and the rack of costumes was pushed up against the bathroom door, so that anyone who wanted to use the toilet had to push the rack in front of one of the occupied mirrors.

The girl, who had introduced herself as Joelle, waved her hand around the room. "Sucks, right?"

It occurred to Diane that most girls trying to propel themselves to her kind of fame had to start out in a place like this, moving furniture to get to the bathroom. But it also occurred to her that if Romey had come across this dancer in a Waffle House, she might have been the Girl from Saint-Mandé instead.

"Well," Diane said, "what's nice about it is that there's no fuss or anything."

Joelle laughed. "What I wouldn't give for fuss."

Rachel grabbed Diane's elbow. "I have the best idea." Her eyes were shining. "You should take Joelle's place for a song."

Diane looked at her. "Like what, go onstage? Very funny."

"Why not? When are you ever going to have another chance to do something like this?"

"Why don't you do it then?"

Rachel shook her pink hair out of her face. "If I didn't have this freakish hair I'd do it in a second. Do you have any wigs, Joelle?"

Joelle shook her head.

"You're the only one of us people might not recognize with a lot of makeup on," Rachel said.

Joelle said, "I'm okay with it if you are. I think it would be awesome."

"But I'm a terrible singer," Diane protested.

"Not everyone sings. There's a track if you want it."

Diane looked pleadingly at Jessica, who had always seemed to her to be the rational one.

But Jessica shrugged. "You should do it. We all know you've been freaking out over that sex scene. Maybe this would help."

"But they'll recognize me," Diane said softly, suddenly realizing they were all serious. "Someone will know me. It'll end up in the tabloids." She thought of the way the girls ran their hands over their bodies as they danced and felt sick at the thought of doing that in front of all those people, when she had so much to lose if they recognized her.

Jessica shook her head. "Never in a million years would anyone think that Diane Hausman would be dancing in a cabaret club in the Village. It's like hiding in plain sight."

Diane thought about Rachel, and how even with her pink hair none of the photographers had noticed her; she was, somehow, just another girl standing on a sidewalk in New York.

Joelle looked at her with wide eyes. "God, haven't you ever wanted to be someone else, though, even for a few minutes?" She seemed to be looking not at Diane but past her, at another life, maybe, one where she was not up at midnight dancing for money in New York, but fast asleep in her childhood bed instead, a college textbook open on her desk, her father snoring down the hall, and the soft sounds of the suburbs washing over her.

◆ ◆ ◆

Once, after her parents died, Diane had come across an old, gray-eared dog who had collapsed on a sidewalk in Morristown. The owner was kneeling on the ground next to the dog, cradling its head in his lap. The dog managed to lift its head enough to lick the man's hand, its pink tongue lolling out of its mouth, panting in such a way that it looked strangely like it was smiling, even though everyone crowded around knew the dog wouldn't make it up again. Diane had wondered if it was possible that dogs, like people, saw angels before they died, and whether this dog was seeing dog angels or people angels, and whether if they took him he would go to dog heaven or people heaven.

Watching the man, it had seemed to Diane that his very existence depended on that dog. He laid his hand on the side of the dog's head and said aloud, with sudden, desperate conviction, "He'll be okay.

He will." And a few moments later, to everyone's disbelief, the dog blinked its dark eyes and struggled to its feet. Everyone clapped and murmured. Man and dog walked off, the dog unsteadily, away from the crowd, the man periodically reaching down to pat the dog's head. It had seemed to Diane, at the time, impossible that such a thing had happened. But then she had been overcome with a kind of awareness that not everything had to be the way you expected. At the surprising, critical moments in her life—meeting Jack, her divorce, standing in the middle of Romey's hotel room—she had found herself thinking of that dog and reminding herself of this truth.

Bound in a stiff silver corset, blinking under the stage lights as the track played its first long, slow notes, she could almost imagine she was back out on the street, caught in the blinding flashbulbs of the paparazzi. The layers of foundation that Joelle had caked on her skin moments before felt dewy under the hot lights. She worried that all the makeup might come undone and slip off her face like a silk mask, suddenly revealing her.

Slowly, she put her heel up on the seat of a wooden chair and slid one stocking down her thigh. She felt the notes of the music falling over her, and as the piano continued playing it occurred to her that despite being an actress, for the first time in her life she really, truly felt like someone else entirely—someone she hadn't met yet but might come across later in life, when these days were behind her, in some ordinary place like a grocery store or a mall—some bright, ordinary woman, with a baby on her hip, perhaps, maybe a little plain or heavy but happy, dancing to the scratchy store music in the middle of the aisle.

From the speakers in the ceiling, Edith Piaf sang, *Entraînée par la foule qui s'élance*—Driven by the crowd that rushes—lyrics Diane remembered from high school French, the songs the only thing she liked about the class. Looking into the crowd, she could see Jessica and Rachel, drinks in their hands. And beyond that, through the tiny window nestled above the lighting booth, she thought she could see that gray dog flying home too, and Jack in his jet, and Levi calling her name from another hemisphere, and surely, she thought, we are all driven by the crowd, and swept away.

Prayers of an American Wife

This is a Navy town at 5 o'clock in the morning: the sun rising in a blaze over the ocean and the first of the jets overhead and two teenagers in the lifeguard stand with their arms around each other. The boardwalk is lined with early runners, strapped with knee bands and water belts, and women who run with spaceship-like strollers, their babies flapping their feet inside tiny, sagging socks. At the inlet, the photographers set their tripods in the surf, squinting at the sleek, gray-winged airplanes slicing through the clouds.

In the North End, while their fathers shave for work, the children are curled in their beds under white summer comforters, because the buses for camp run at 8 and their dreams are still full of colored horses and storms that wash over the beach like small baptisms. Farther inland, on the air base, the mechanics perform safety checks while the pilots brief upstairs in front of whiteboards and tabletops crowded with plastic jets on wooden dowels. Nothing else is open yet this early except the golf course and the front gate and Tim Hortons. Even the Officers' Club is still dark. The woman who mops the floors in the morning likes to think of the place full of life, when Phyllis hurries back and forth behind the bar and knows everyone's drink orders and even the ages of their children. In a glass case by the door is an inconspicuous nametag that reads "Goose," the call sign of a pilot who died in Miramar while *Top Gun* was being filmed, because the greatest fictions always come from real life.

And this is a Navy town, too, in the pink-washed morning—past the beaches and the wide white houses, past the arcades and the hotels with striped towels drying on the railings—this is the sun coming up over the airfield, and three miles south of base, where land is cheaper and plots are larger, this is the neighborhood where the officers buy houses when they marry, where their new wives contemplate babies and hand-scraped floors and espresso makers. This is the neighborhood where the pilots will love their wives for the last time before they deploy, where they won't think about who will wash the cars while they are gone, but they will think about the moonless black nights on the carrier, they will think about the 130-odd times they will land their jets at sea in those dark nights. They will think how it never gets any easier.

And this is where Mack's twenty-six-year-old wife, Alissa, crouches in the dark by the bathroom window, watching her neighbor's house for signs of a man sneaking out.

His name isn't really Mack. That's only what he's known as—not because he was ever very good with women ("Mack *daddy!*" he liked to say), but because on a detachment to Key West he got a bad mackerel and puked on some pretty girl. For squadron events Alissa sometimes wears a T-shirt that says *Lady Mack*, and everyone loves it. She has always called him Mack, she has never called him Bill, because when she met him while she was still in nursing school, he was already Mack to everyone, and he had already been to the Gulf twice, and he seemed very old those nights when they stood out on the pier with the ocean spread out like a plum-black tablecloth in front of them.

Across the lawn, she can see a light on in Beth's house and the shadow of someone moving around in the bedroom behind the curtains. She can't tell if there are two people in the room; she suspects there are. She has suspected this for weeks, ever since Beth's husband left with Mack for Afghanistan and she saw a strange car in the cul-de-sac a few nights later. Alissa saw the dark head of a man climbing the steps onto her own porch and fumbling under her mat as if looking for a key—and then, as she searched in the closet for the gun, she saw him walk next door to Beth's house.

The next day, out in the yard with Brady, the orange Pomeranian Mack bought her before he left, sniffing around at her heels, she saw Beth through the fence. "Someone came to my door last night," she called over. "I think he thought my house was your house."

Beth laughed a little. "Oh, yeah, my brother. He's in town."

"Is he staying with you?" Alissa bent over to pick a weed from the edge of the manicured lawn.

"At a hotel. He wants to stay by the beach." Beth hesitated. "Sorry if he woke you up."

Alissa shook her head. "No, it's okay. I was up."

Now she is up again, early, watching for the man's return. When a brother didn't appear the following day, she knew Beth had been lying. A week later she found a beer bottle tossed into the sewer in front of Beth's driveway—nothing so scandalous and incriminating as a condom, but still.

She isn't sure why she feels so protective of Beth's husband, Paul—he has never been particularly friendly to Mack, even though they fly in the same squadron—but for some reason she thinks that if it was Mack who was cheating, Beth's husband would be at the window too, looking out for Alissa.

She can't tell anyone, of course, not during the deployment. But afterward, what then? When the men get home, will Beth already be gone? She has heard of wives who flee with the children and all the money—even with classified information. There was a case once of an Iranian college student—the fiancée of a Hornet pilot—funneling intelligence back to her country. This cautionary tale has been spreading in the community for years, and when you marry someone with security clearances now you too are screened closely by the government, by an agent who comes into your home and glances at the titles of the books on your shelves.

It has occurred to her that Paul might be cheating on Beth as well. Deployments are nothing but long stretches of time, and there are plenty of women out there.

Alissa has spent the night contemplating her own code with Beth, not sure if there even is one. When she and Mack bought the house, Beth came over with a large bouquet of flowers—not a limp, plastic-wrapped one from Harris Teeter, but sturdy white roses arranged in a wicker basket, like a painting from an Italian art book. Alissa forgave her then for having dated Mack, for having been the one everyone said he would marry—*Mackbeth*—everyone used to laugh hilariously at this—*oh, I have given suck, and know!*—and for the way Beth touched his shoulder once as she pushed past him at a crowded party, a familiarity she no longer had any right to.

After they split up, he met Alissa, who he met in the ER when he
got in a fight and broke his jaw, and he saw the kind of wife you
had to have if you flew jets and sometimes came home after a bad
landing with the hot sweat of the cockpit inside your shirt, he saw
that in your bed you would want someone as composed as that,
someone who knew what a lot of blood looked like.

They got married on the beach after only three months, by a priest
Beth had been friends with since they were children together, and
there had been a honeymoon to Williamsburg and then the long wait
in a white-tiled hallway to receive her pink dependent's ID card. Two
months later Beth married Paul.

In the blue dark of the early morning, as Alissa watches the light
go on in Beth's bathroom, her phone rings from upstairs, on the
nightstand where she left it. The dog whines from his crate as she
sprints to the bedroom, arriving breathless at the edge of the bed.
"Mack? Is that you?" She hears nothing for a moment—the delay
of a censored line.

"Hey, Liss." His response is soft and faraway, like something
played on someone else's radio. "We're about to go into a blackout
here, I might be cut off. Is everything okay?"

"Yeah, it's fine." She takes the phone downstairs to her bathroom
post. "Have you gotten—there yet?" She can't name countries on
the phone.

Mack still sounds far away. "Yeah."

It seems suddenly, crucially important to know if Beth's husband
is cheating too. "Has Paul talked to Beth lately?" she asks.

"I dunno, why? Is something wrong?"

"No, no, I just didn't want to tell her you called me if he hasn't
been calling her."

"Whatever. If he's not calling and she gets mad, that's their problem."

"Yeah, I know."

"How's Brady?"

"He misses you. He stands at the door at night waiting for you to
come home from work."

"That's terrible."

"Yeah. I've been trying to find another dog for him."

She hears voices in the background. "Shit, I gotta go," he says suddenly. "Sorry, I'll call you later. I love you."

When he hangs up she stares at the blue screen on her phone like it's a portal she could walk through to get somewhere else.

Outside, through the open window, she hears the rustle of a bush in Beth's yard. She gets to her feet. But when she looks out the window, no one is there.

◆ ◆ ◆

It's a strange existence when the men are gone. There isn't a reason, really, to go on base anymore, since almost everyone lives in houses outside the gates, although once a month the wives get together in someone's dining room and talk about care packages and home-coming, even though it is still seven months and practically three seasons away.

There are secrets that need to be kept from the other wives, things Mack has told her about their husbands, and it is sometimes hard to separate her dislike for some of those men—for their cruel hazing of the new guys or their cheating or the weed they smoke before flying—from how she feels about the women who married them. It is harder, too, to forget that some of these women are the wives of her husband's bosses, and jobs have been won or lost on the merits of a pilot's spouse. So she always dresses nicely for these dinners, remembers everyone's birthday, and never gossips about another wife. Her college friends—who are mostly nurses or doctors or lawyers who moved north instead of south when they graduated—don't understand any of it.

Then there is a kind of loss of identity that comes after the men leave. It feels almost like a kind of death, although none of them will say this. But after the sea bags and suitcases are loaded onto the carrier, the guys simply go to work with their flight bags like any other day, climb into the jet like any other flight, but this time they don't come home at the end of the night, and the wives are left to empty the refrigerator of all the foods their husbands like, and to wash the last dirty T-shirts, and to empty the garage of anything useless and throw out files that aren't needed anymore. And when all of this is done there is very little left to do if you don't have children yet, and you foresee long stretches of evenings reading novels on the deck or watching movies, and you will have to find an identity beyond that of a wife, you will have to join a tennis league or start going to church. Some women train for marathons, or go on diets, or take art classes, but really they are all trying to do the same thing—they are trying to emerge somehow more cultured or more beautiful than when their husbands left, and at the same time they are trying to live as if there is no one they are waiting for.

◆ ◆ ◆

For the next three nights Alissa is off from the hospital, and from 10 till midnight and dawn till 7, she watches Beth's house for signs of the dark-haired man. On the third night she is certain she hears the laughter of two people on the back deck, but no one comes into view, and eventually she falls asleep on the soft yellow bathmat with Brady on her feet.

The morning after that third night, when she thinks she hears voices next door, she wakes up exhausted. She can't quite understand what kind of cold fear grips her when she settles down to stand guard over Beth's house. It has occurred to her that maybe these vigils are masking her own insecurities about Mack, that she too, like the other wives, worries that something will happen while he's gone—that he'll cheat or crash or something—and that if he comes home again it will all be different, that they won't be as in love as they were when he left, or he'll be distracted or controlling or have PTSD, or the small joys of their small life won't be enough for him anymore.

She takes Brady over to Beth's house on Saturday morning and stands on the porch, wondering if she's imagining the whole thing. Beth answers the door in a pair of sweatpants and a T-shirt, although, because she's a true southern-bred woman, her hair and makeup have been carefully done.

"Do you want to walk with us?" Alissa asks, motioning at Brady, who is trying to jump into Beth's arms from his position at her knees.

Beth looks surprised. She glances back into the house and then down at her bare feet. "Okay. Let me just get my sneakers." She leans down and pats Brady's head before she ducks back inside.

On the long stretch of sidewalk, they talk about Brady and then their husbands for a while, and Alissa searches Beth's comments for something telling, something about the marriage falling apart, but there is nothing.

They stop at a crosswalk where, on the other side, a man on a bike is waiting for the light next to a young girl, and the idea hangs between them that children are the next reasonable part of life to happen. Alissa tries to imagine her life five, ten years in the future, waking to the noises of a baby on some distant base in some hot, chalky stretch of country.

She is overtaken by an awareness of how fast life goes, how it wasn't even long ago that she spent her Saturdays biking down the boardwalk with her own father, her sandals slapping loudly against the pedals, and then, as if in the course of a few weeks, she was grown up with a job and married. Her parents had retired to an affordable coastal town in North Carolina. It seems urgent to her suddenly that she convey this realization to Beth, that Beth understand how critical and fleeting time is, how much is at stake in every decision.

"Did you have someone over last night?" Alissa asks her, without preface. She knows she should try to be less direct, but she can't think of any other way to ask it.

Beth looks at her strangely. "No. Why?"

Alissa is taken aback by how convincing Beth's response is. She wonders, alarmed, if she really has imagined it all. She laughs. "Oh, never mind. I thought I heard you outside, that's all. It was so nice out last night."

Beth reaches down to untangle Brady's leash from around her legs. "It must have been the TV. I was watching a movie. Sorry—I'll close the door to the deck next time."

They turn onto another street, neither of them saying anything. A group of high school girls passes them, jogging in sports bras and neon sneakers. Finally Beth turns to her. "Actually, I wanted to tell you something."

Alissa looks at her. "Tell me what?"

"That we're selling the house."

"You are?"

"Paul called me last night. His orders came in early. He's coming home in three weeks."

"But he almost just left!"

"I know. He's really crushed about it, actually—no one likes leaving all the guys behind like that. But that's the way it goes, I guess. His time was almost up anyway. And he did the whole last deployment with this squadron."

"Where are you going?"

"California." She scrunches up her nose. "Lemoore. I know I should be happy that it's a good job for Paul, but it's in the middle of nowhere." She looks like she is about to cry.

Alissa reaches for her arm. "And—you're going with him for sure?"

She senses the slightest—just the slightest—hint of a pause in Beth's response. "Why wouldn't I?" Beth smiles, like a good southern girl. "Don't worry. I'll try to pick some good neighbors for you."

◆ ◆ ◆

The rest of the week passes with no sign of the man. Alissa cuts her vigil down to an hour after dinner when she's not working.

Then, one evening in the early days of June, she sees him again, making his way around the back of Beth's house to the side door. And there is Beth, a glimpse of a blue dress in the doorway, ushering him inside. Alissa kneels in the dark in her bathroom as if in prayer, the soft, slight dripping of the sink behind her, clutching Brady to her chest. He squirms in her arms, unaware of the betrayal happening just across the lawn.

It surprises her, her reaction. She is not proud of her discovery, or reassured, or relieved. Instead she is utterly, savagely heartbroken, and she can't bring herself to get up off the bathroom floor. It seems to her as if everything she's believed in—the sanctity of her own marriage with Mack, the certainty that people are generally good—has been shattered.

But there is no uncertainty now about the situation. She pulls on her sneakers and slips quietly into the backyard, where she has a better view of Beth's house, and there—unmistakably, in the bedroom window—is Beth's bright, lamp-lit body, wrapped in the arms of Paul and Mack's old flight instructor Alan Greene.

✦ ✦ ✦

She goes to Mass the following morning to see Father Rob, the priest who married her, who grew up down the street from her on the west side of town.

Rob is the assistant rector of an Episcopal church that sits on a hill a block from the ocean, in the wealthier North End of the city. Alissa has always loved the cream-painted walls and the silvered views of the sea through the tall stained-glass windows. Rob joined the Marines after college, but he was medically discharged after only a year, for a kidney condition the government didn't want to pay for, and it was funny because he had started thinking about God, he said, not in Iraq or anything like that—in fact he had never even been deployed—but in the white, thin-walled rooms of the barracks where, while doing a routine check on one of the buildings, he overheard a private praying in the room next door. The kid was eighteen and just out of high school—Rob knew him, he was heavy and friendless—and it sounded like he was trying to say the Our Father but didn't know all the words. The next day Rob caught him drinking from a flask of alcohol while on duty, and the guy didn't fight his dismissal at all, just sat in the office with stooped shoulders and a tired, tragic look of failure in his eyes.

It is still strange to Alissa to see the boy she played kick the can with standing in the front of a congregation in his white robes, bowing over a chalice of wine. He seems blessed with something, even though he is also someone she saw naked once during a high school dare, even though she knows that he has struggled to find love as a single priest in a marriageable religion, and that he has his own insecurities about being a priest in a military town when he couldn't finish his own years of service.

He smiles at her during Communion as she kneels in front of him. He places the wafer into her open palms and says, "God be with you" before moving on to the elderly woman beside her. After the reception that always follows the Sunday Mass, he leads her into his office and loosens his collar as he sits down on the couch. She sits next to him and when his robe is off and he is sitting beside her in his khaki pants and white shirt, like the kid she used to sit next to at church, she leans back, slips off her shoes, and pulls her knees up to her chest.

"So what's up?" he asks, in that casual way they always speak to each other. "I feel like I haven't seen you in forever."

She says, "I feel like I'm losing my mind."

He frowns. "Is it Mack?" She knows Rob has never liked Mack much.

She shakes her head. "No, nothing like that. It's my neighbor—you know, that girl who dated him before me."

"Yeah, I remember."

"She's cheating on her husband."

"Oh," Rob says heavily. "Are you sure?"

Alissa nods. "I saw them. It's been going on for a while, I think. He parks somewhere else and then walks to the house so nobody notices his car out front."

"Do you know the guy?"

She nods. "It's their old training instructor." It is the gravest sin, in the military, to steal the wife of someone you once worked with. It is an unforgivable sin. "Do I tell Mack?"

Rob shakes his head. "No, I don't think so." He closes his blue eyes thoughtfully. "I don't think you should."

"Her husband's coming home in two weeks. She says they're moving to California."

"Is she going?"

"She says she is. I don't understand why she would, though, if she doesn't even want to be with him."

He hesitates. "Maybe it's not that simple."

She knows he is referring to her father—to that afternoon, all those years ago, when they saw him kissing another woman in a parking lot near Rob's house. But they never told her mother, and her father never left, and they never saw the woman again. And she knows her parents are happy now—they still go grocery shopping together every Sunday. But she can't seem to reconcile the man he appears to be with the one who once held another woman in his arms.

"I think you should let it go," Rob says. "It's not your battle to fight."

She shakes her head. "If you weren't a priest and you didn't feel like you had to say that, what would you really tell me?"

He laughs, and she sees a flicker of the old Rob in him. "I'd tell you nothing you do is gonna change the outcome."

"That's not true. I can tell her husband."

"Don't put yourself in the middle of other people's unhappiness."

She glares at him. "Isn't that what you do every day?"

"Hey," he says. "Don't take it out on me."

When Rob first told her he was entering the seminary—before she met Mack, when she was still in nursing school—she felt a strong wash of sadness, not really a sense of loss but a sense of being left behind somehow. It was as if he had realized some truth that most people spend their whole lives trying to understand—and only the lucky ones manage it.

"I miss you," she says quietly, putting her head on his shoulder. "We used to do everything together."

He rests his hand on her ponytail. "I haven't gone anywhere."

But he has—he's gone into the Episcopal Church—and she's gone too, into the kind of messy secular life, with its alcohol and pettiness and profanities, that he will always stand apart from. And one day Mack will get orders for his shore tour and they'll go somewhere else, like Nevada or Tennessee, and she'll have no reason to come back here, and Rob will slowly drift out of her life, become someone she knew once in her twenties, someone she sends cards to at Christmas. She isn't in love with him romantically; but he is, to her, that rare person who has been a witness to her life—not just the life that started when she met Mack, but her whole life—and he is someone she can look at and say, *He knew me then, in the beginning.* She thinks, for all his relationship with God, that he needs another person to see him this way too.

He puts his arm around her, and they sit there in silence until the secretary knocks on the door, and Alissa slips her shoes back on and stands up to leave.

* * *

After that afternoon she stops watching for Alan Greene. She knows he still comes to the house; she hears his car on quiet nights as he drives slowly down the street, as if to check that Beth is home, and then out of the cul-de-sac again to wherever it is he parks. She doesn't tell Mack about Alan, though.

A few weeks later she adopts a female terrier named Cricket from a shelter in Town Center, and she does tell Mack about this, and about how Brady doesn't wait for him at the door anymore, but falls asleep with his head on Cricket's back, at the foot of the bed. Mack asks about the puppy with longing in his voice, as if she's a baby he hasn't met yet.

Beth's house is put up for sale, and a steady stream of potential buyers drive in and out of the neighborhood to view the property. Then, in early July, the day before Paul is scheduled to fly home on the airlift, something unexpected happens—Alan Greene comes to Beth's house in full daylight. He parks right in the driveway: the first time, as far as Alissa is aware, that he's ever done this. She sees him just as she is about to take the dogs out. At first she thinks he's another buyer, but then she sees his close-shaved head as he climbs out of the car in his flight suit and heavy boots. The dogs are pawing at the door and whining, and she pulls them back and stands in the half-open doorway, holding her breath. He doesn't go up to the house, only stands at the end of the driveway, looking up at the darkened windows. Then he takes something out of his pocket, slips it into the mailbox, and gets back in his car.

Brady is yanking on the leash. She wonders whether—if Rob were the one living here—even he would have enough self-restraint to shut the door again and turn on the television and stay inside the house. Instead, she picks up her cell phone and sends Beth a message. *Are you home? Do you need any help with the house?*

Beth writes back a minute later. *I'm okay, thanks. Out looking for shoes.*

She lets the dogs into the side yard and hurries across the front lawn. Her heart is beating like a bird in her chest. Somewhere out there, she thinks, Beth is trying on the shoes she will greet her husband in, and Paul knows nothing about what's going on.

Alan hasn't sealed the note. It's written on a piece of computer paper and folded into thirds. *I'm begging you not to go*, it says, the handwriting small and cramped. *Tell him tomorrow.* The words take up only one line, and the rest of the page is blank. Alissa stands in the street, holding the letter, knowing that if she throws it away, if Beth never sees it, thirty years from now Beth and Paul could be just like her parents, walking down the aisles of the Safeway together, as far away from this day as they could ever be.

♦ ♦ ♦

When Paul comes home, he doesn't have the kind of welcome the other men will at the end—the spouses and photographers lined up on the airfield, the cake and champagne in the hangar—just Beth waiting for him on the pavement in a new dress. Alissa hears Beth's garage door open as she leaves in the morning. When she returns with Paul a few hours later, they park in front of the garage and walk up the steps together, laughing and holding hands.

Even though she knows there are problems between them—without knowing what specific words or violence they can't take back—Alissa can't help feeling envious as they lie outside on their deck chairs later that afternoon, lounging in the July sun. In the privacy of her own deck, separated from theirs by the tall wooden fence, she can't quite make out their conversation, but the quiet intimacy of the moment has made its mark on her.

The strange soundlessness of the hot season is, she thinks, something unique to this place. For a month or so each year, everything living outside sleeps or dies; nothing stirs. Still, she was married in this kind of weather the summer before. She remembers the flash of the new gold on her finger and the brassy notes of the band on the lawn. In the background, somewhere, was Rob; in the background, Beth and Paul danced with each other.

She wonders if Beth ever responded to Alan's note.

Later that night, around dinnertime, she hears a car engine outside. The dogs race to the door. She senses something is wrong and goes to the window, alarmed, to see Beth driving out of the cul-de-sac. Paul isn't with her. Alissa runs out to the road in time to see the car turn the corner, Beth's long blond hair streaming out the open window.

She stands there in the middle of the street, wondering if Beth has really left Paul after all. But she doesn't see Paul storming out behind the car, or even watching through the window. It is possible, she thinks, that Beth didn't tell Paul anything at all. It is possible she said she was going to the grocery store and won't come back again, that she will call Paul from some hotel on the far side of town.

Then, surprisingly, Alissa looks up to see the flash of a pair of headlights at the end of the road. It's Beth's car. She hasn't turned the corner after all; she's turned the car around. She's driving slowly back down the street, one hand on the steering wheel and the other gripping the bottom of the open window.

As she comes back down the street, Beth sees her and lifts her free hand to wave. She looks extraordinarily calm. "Oh, hi," Beth calls out. "I was just on my way home."

The Strangers of Dubai

The war seemed far away from the hot, dusty room inside the gold market. Outside in the street, clusters of robed women huddled like pigeons, and you couldn't tell who was Western and who was Eastern beneath the fabric, who was skinny or rich or beautiful or only wishing to be. The shopkeepers stood at attention in the doorways, like butlers, and tried to identify the richest Indian brides, the ones whose mothers cooed over wedding sets studded with emeralds.

My husband was happiest that weekend floating in the hotel pool, watched by waiters who hovered with cold towels and glided back and forth to a bar stocked with watermelon juice. It was nothing like the ship: the too-narrow staterooms and the toilets that wouldn't flush, the jets pounding the decks, and the way you sometimes in the red-lit darkness couldn't tell whether it was day or night. But in the hotel, there were marble baths and the hall lights and air-conditioning stayed on all night.

In the market we quickly discovered that gold is expensive wherever you go, and we wandered into a side street shop to buy cheaper souvenirs instead. Two shopkeepers, dressed in white, stood side by side with their hands clasped behind their backs. I pointed to a wall of silk pashminas. "How much are these?"

One of the men stepped forward. He was younger than the other, but I guessed that the older one didn't know English. "Three hundred dirham," he said—about $30.

My husband shook his head. "One hundred," he countered.

The younger one looked at the older man and said something I couldn't understand. The older man nodded almost imperceptibly and shuffled into the back while the younger watched us, amused. "You are American?" he asked.

We were stationed in Virginia at the time, living in a townhouse two blocks from the beach. But my husband, holding me tightly by the waist, smiled as if he didn't understand.

The man smiled back at us, a tight-lipped smile, as if we were all playing the same game. He was young, no more than twenty-five. "I am from Afghanistan," he said, still smiling, and I understood that my husband had already known this, that he had recognized in the men's speech words he had heard before. But before any of us could speak again the pashminas were brought in. They were wrapped in cellophane, the fabrics inside as delicate as stockings and brightly colored, like birds.

My husband took out his credit card.

"No card," the young man said. "Dirham."

"I only have the card."

"We take you to cash machine."

My husband hesitated. He had been on the ground with men just like these, men who smiled at him but shot rockets over the wall of the compound at night. And none of us knew now in this neutral desert whether we were friends or enemies or what the others had or hadn't done.

The men pushed the pashminas into a plastic bag and led us out of the shop and down the street into a private courtyard, where groups of more white-smocked men stood around smoking.

The younger shopkeeper gestured to an ATM pushed against the wall of a shuttered bank. "Here is cash," he said, then stuck out his chin when my husband didn't move. "You get cash," he said again, forcefully this time. He edged us both forward, and I could smell the dry sootiness of his breath on my neck. My husband opened his wallet and the other shopkeeper pushed forward as well, so that all four of us were pressed together in front of the machine. I could hardly breathe, and I wished I hadn't insisted we go shopping.

But when I followed my husband's gaze, I saw that our shopkeepers weren't looking at us. They were looking at the smoking men, who were eyeing us eagerly. It only then occurred to me that our shopkeepers had formed a wall behind us so that these men couldn't do whatever it was they had hoped to do.

When the cash slid out of the machine, the older man put out his hand. He took the money and put it in his pocket and held out his hand again. When my husband put out his hand as well, I understood that it was not more money that was being asked for.

They grasped each other's palms.

"This good buy," the younger man translated, gesturing toward the pashminas.

"Yes." My husband repeated. "It's goodbye."

The Whispering Gallery

She was in London alone for the summer, in St Paul's Cathedral. The doors of the church were open, and the smell of fish batter and oiled newspaper poured into the building from the street carts. Mixed with the incense, it made her feel slightly sick. This was not exactly as she had remembered the cathedral.

In the Whispering Gallery, under the dome, ninety-nine feet above the cathedral's altar, it was said a person could whisper into any part of the circular wall and be heard a hundred feet away, on the opposite side of the circle. Her father had told her this nineteen years ago, in 1987, when they had flown from Pensacola with her mother because her father had always dreamed of taking them to London. He had done six years of odd jobs to pay for the four-day trip; but her mother, uninterested in churches, stayed behind at the hotel that day.

"Go on, say something to me," her father had prodded her in the gallery, and she had been sent around to the other side. Just beyond the railing lay the massive cavernous space above the nave, and the narrow ring of ledge that comprised the gallery was crowded, people pushing, everyone pushing to tell their secrets to the wall. Tourists pressed in on her, so that she found herself crushed against the cold stone, and immediately she heard a rush of whispers, like a flock of birds, and then she had heard her father's voice—*Nicole*—as if he had been standing right beside her. *Nicole. Come back.* She straightened, startled, and when she turned she saw him waving at her, telling her to hurry.

"We've got to go," he said when she returned. "It's later than I thought. It's time for me to take your mom out on our date."

"I could hear you!" She grinned, then frowned. "I didn't get to say anything to you though."

They had rushed back to the hotel to meet her mother, and her parents had put her to bed and gone in a cab to dinner. And they had not come back. Her aunt had flown over from Florida in a black dress with bows on the sleeves and taken her from the police station in Chelsea to Heathrow airport, to the small resort community of Destin.

✦ ✦ ✦

She was twenty-eight years old now, back in London for the first time since then. It was a Wednesday morning and the church was quiet. The colors of the day slipped through the highest little windows, and the whole space seemed, aside from the smells, as still as a dollhouse and relatively unchanged.

Ever since the accident, all memories of her childhood had sounded like echoes to her, and looked like little jewel-colored saints set into stained glass. Memory in its entirety seemed to have been ravaged by that day. But now she also recalled what she had heard about the cathedral being protected by angels; it had remained untouched during the Blitz of 1941, though the bombs had devastated the city around it. Thinking about this and about her father, she half expected, for a moment, to see him on the other side of the Whispering Gallery across from her, wearing the same red sweater. She half expected his voice to be inside the wall still, and if she put her ear to the stone again, she would hear him. It wasn't impossible. She had read about messages being delivered through walls. In Israel, a son had found his deceased father's prayer stuffed into the Western Wall. But there were no voices for her. There was only an older couple far off, their heads buried in a pamphlet.

When she finally turned around, it wasn't her father she saw, it was Andy. Andy in a pair of black suit pants and a suit jacket, on the far side of the gallery. He had his back to her.

What was he doing here? What was he doing in that ridiculous wool jacket in summer? She was angry with him at first. This was *her father's* place, not his, and he had trespassed on something private. She and Andy had had their own private places—the dock, the beach near Pensacola Air Station. But showing up like this, here of all places... He liked to watch her from a distance—from the back of a movie theater, or a swing set in the park—just to make sure she was all right. When she saw him in these places he smiled at her, so that she knew he had seen her.

But he had never come to watch her in a church, which was the last place she had ever spoken to him or touched him. Of course, he hadn't been able to answer her then—his lower half ravaged by the war, the casket closed from the waist down—but somehow she had known he would not leave her for good, not when she had already suffered that kind of loss once.

But now Andy was facing away from her, which made her uneasy, as if he had his own reasons to be in this place that didn't have to do with her. She made her way around the ledge toward him. He had his head against the wall and one hand stretched above it, the palm flat against the stone, as if in some kind of awkward prayer. He didn't seem to notice she was there. What was he doing here? She was breathless by now; she had not been this close to him in a long time.

She reached out and touched his wrist, and he turned around. Her first thought was, *He's so much older!* There were lines in his forehead. Then, to her horror, she realized it wasn't actually Andy at all. It was Richard.

She choked, wishing he would turn around again, wishing he would step back into the minute before so he could be Andy still.

"Nicole? What are you doing here? My *God!*" He reached out to hug her, and she stumbled backward.

"That jacket," she said, pointing. "It's Andy's. I thought you were—"

He looked down at the faded wool and frowned. "Oh, no. I'm so sorry. I didn't expect to see—"

"Of course not." She caught her breath and tried to laugh. She didn't want to appear fragile or desperate, in front of Richard of all people. *Of course* he was wearing Andy's jacket; closets full of clothes didn't disappear when people died. It was silly to think Richard wouldn't have kept at least one of his brother's things.

"It's been—a long time, hasn't it?" she said. She had grown up since then—darkened her hair and changed the way she dressed and how she spoke. She wasn't some poor girl from the backwoods of

Florida anymore. She had a library card and health insurance and a master's degree.

Her eyes drifted back to his jacket. "It's hot out, though, for something like that, isn't it?"

He smiled, holding out the sleeves as if to examine them. "Oh," he said. "Well, you know London. Yesterday they were calling for cold. I'm on my way back to the airport, so I've got to lug this heavy thing along now."

"Are you on vacation?" she asked.

He shook his head. "Business. I live in Dublin now. Dad's moved his company over there, you know."

"I didn't know."

Richard's face reddened. "I'm sorry. That was stupid. I don't know why I thought. . ."

"It's all right."

"I just flew over for the day, and I thought I'd stop in here before I went back." He looked around. The light from the windows settled on his hair, washing the black in purple. He *looked* Irish, with his gas-blue eyes and dark hair. "I like it here. It's peaceful."

"Yes," she said. "It's quiet today." There was no one else in the gallery now.

He glanced behind her. "Are you here alone?" he asked, as if to really say, *Are you seeing anyone? Have you married?* but she ignored this part of the question and simply nodded.

"And you're on vacation?" he asked.

"Yes. My father brought me here, a long time ago. I was wondering whether it had changed."

"Has it?"

"It smells different," she said. "Not as—churchy." She wanted to kick herself for saying that.

He laughed. She wondered whether Andy had ever told him about her father. "It smells like tourists," he said. "That fish and chips crap. The cheap stuff is all over the city now, but it's fake, you know, they make it different on the street than in the pubs."

There was a long silence, and then finally Richard looked away and lowered his voice. "Listen, it's funny I ran into you. I was going to call you. . ."

36

"Oh?" They had had almost no contact in nearly five years.

"I assume you've been contacted—about the article?"

Of course he would bring that up, right off the bat like that. He was never one for small talk or courtesies. She looked at him suspiciously; could he have followed her here? But of course, that was silly, and also impossible. How would he have known she was even in London? Still, it was strange for them to meet like this—just when that journalist had come sniffing around, asking questions about Andy's medal. He was trying, he said, to determine whether Andy *had* actually been alive after the plane crashed, whether he *had* actually thrown himself in front of that other officer when the gunfire came. He had reason to believe, he said, that Andy had died on impact . . . He had called her, offering payment for an interview; he wanted to get a sense of the man Andy was, and who knew better than her?

What happened, she had been told after Andy's death, was that some helicopter had crashed in Afghanistan. Andy was flying the Chinook that carried the rescue team, but they too had been shot at and they had all died in the crash, except for Andy and one other. Andy, barely breathing, had crawled from the cockpit and fought off a group of insurgents on the ground, until he too was killed—though the one he saved got away.

The one came to talk to her once, and told her Andy had kept her picture on the inside of his flight suit. And then Andy had earned the Navy Cross posthumously.

But now, five years later, that journalist started asking questions, got the surviving officer to admit he may *not* have remembered the story correctly. . . . He had been injured at the time, he wasn't sure, his memory was vague. . . it was possible Andy had actually died in the crash after all, thrown from the cockpit.

In the cathedral, Richard was watching Nicole impatiently. "Are you going to talk to that reporter?" he asked her finally.

"I don't know." Nicole hesitated.

Richard sighed. "If it's about money—"

"I'm *not* doing it for the money." She took a step backward.

He was exactly as she remembered him. *Richard Cook*—it had to be *Richard*, of course, not Ricky or Rich—standing there in his three-piece suit with Andy's old sports jacket thrown over it, trying to seem like he wasn't trying too hard, swearing now and then to seem young still, and rebellious. He was nothing like Andy. What he'd done to her was almost unforgivable. Andy would never have wanted it to happen that way.

"I'm sorry." Richard held up his hand. "I didn't mean anything by that. It's just that I don't want anything to do with it, that's all. It's been five years, and—" He hesitated. "And everything's different." He looked at his watch. His hand was trembling; was he nervous? It startled her, how unlike him it was, and he shoved it back into the pocket of Andy's jacket. "Listen," he said, "I've got to be back in Dublin by this afternoon."

At first she was relieved, then disappointed, although she couldn't imagine the two of them at dinner together, heads bowed in some candle-lit restaurant in Soho, waiting for the intermezzo. But then again, they had met here in such a funny way, stumbling across each other like this, a thousand miles away from where they had buried Andy. It was difficult to let the moment go and say it had meant nothing.

"Well," she said because it was all she could think of. "It was nice to see you."

Richard cleared his throat. "This is going to sound very forward of me, but—you're on vacation, right? Do you want to come to Dublin and see where I live? You could stay over for dinner."

"You mean fly there? To Ireland." She laughed.

"Yes. The flight's just over an hour. And I'd pay for your ticket."

She didn't say anything, and he sighed, obviously impatient with her. They had never gotten along. She knew he was only asking her over to talk her out of doing the interview—the family must be prominent people in Dublin now, and didn't want any kind of scandal—but suddenly Richard looked away, bit hard on his lip. "It would be nice," he said, very softly, "to see you longer."

He unnerved her like this. She had never seen him unsure or afraid, not even after his brother's death, and he seemed suddenly small and worn out. He looked so much like Andy on the night he told her he had to go away. They had the exact same eyes.

"You won't have to see my parents," he continued. "They're in Zurich until Monday."

She hesitated. Before, she would never have considered it. But now, part of her wanted to show Richard how she had made something of herself, in spite of him, in spite of everything. And, too, there seemed to be something good in him, something that reminded her a little of Andy. . . Their meeting was such a coincidence; she couldn't help but wonder if somehow Andy had orchestrated it.

"I've got my bags at the hotel. . ." she began. "I don't know if—"

"Of course." Richard straightened himself, fumbling for his wallet, still careful not to look at her. He hurried to finish. "Listen, I've got to go, but if you decide to come, there's a flight at 4. If you call this number, the agency will give you your reservation code. I'll have a car for you when you get there."

And then, before he left, he looked down at her at last, and, very brazenly, touched the side of her face with his thumb.

She could not bring herself to move. It was the last gesture Andy had made—after the kiss, the exchange of letters—before he had boarded his ship off the coast of Jacksonville. Richard could never have known this.

When Richard left, she stayed in the spot where he had been for a long time, kneeling on the stone floor with her head against the wall, until someone came and asked her if she was all right.

◆ ◆ ◆

On the plane over the Irish Sea, the glare was so bright she had to close the window shade halfway, and her seatmate on the aisle looked over from his book, annoyed. Instead of ignoring him, she opened the shade again and put her head in her hands. She almost couldn't believe what she was doing; this was not the trip she had planned. A week in London—a little sightseeing and a spa. It was the first vacation she had ever taken alone; she'd been so proud of herself. But she was already leaving, to follow a man she didn't even like, of all things.

Richard was still like a stranger to her—they had met only two months before Andy went overseas. She was afraid he may have heard what had become of her since then, but whether it would disgust him or intrigue him, she wasn't sure. She didn't know him well enough for that. And now, after everything, she would sit and share a meal with him, in his home, as if they were friends, as if she was the kind of woman who ran with him in those circles.

It had nothing to do with money, she'd told herself, but of course it all came down to that. News of Andy's death had come three months before their wedding, and when the insurance had been determined ($300,000), she'd had no legal right to it—although before he went away he had designated her as his beneficiary. After all, she was going to be his wife, he'd said; they had known each other for a year and been engaged for half of that time. But then some kind of logistical error had occurred—because she was *not*, in fact, his wife, the money had gone instead to Andy's parents, who had given her nothing but instead invested it all into the company.

Andy was the only man she had ever loved, other than her father. He had beautiful white teeth and robin's egg–blue eyes, and on their first date, he had stood nervously on her apartment steps with an armful of yellow roses. He was not the kind of man to ask to come inside afterward. *I want to take care of you,* he had said.

It hadn't occurred to her that at the funeral she would not be given the flag. So when the moment came—the soldiers standing in white with square faces, like mannequins—the flag was folded and placed in his mother's hands—that *woman's* hands!—it was as if someone had struck her. This was the moment she realized that it was as if her life with Andy had never existed; there was no record of their ever having been together. She did not have his last name; she would not be receiving his benefits; she must leave their house on the base within a week. At the funeral, Andy's mother had put her arm through Nicole's, and afterward there had been light kisses on the cheek before the family's departure for New York.

She blamed Richard for letting it happen. He was Andy's *brother*; he should have been on her side. He was not an ignorant child; he had been a grown man of thirty at the time, CFO of his father's business, while she had $40,000 of college loans to pay, no home, and an aunt in a life-care facility in Destin. When she met Andy, Nicole had quit her job as an advertising assistant to move to southern Florida with him, where no one wanted to hire a Navy spouse who would be relocating in only a couple of years.

Richard had seen, clearly, that Andy's death had shattered her.

She had given all of herself to Andy, and this family—who should have been *her* family—had taken what she desperately needed in order to build an empire from what was already a kingdom. And she had loved him so much. . . . She remembered trying to explain this to Richard; he had stayed a day longer than his parents to help her pack her things and load the truck. But he didn't ask where she was going, and she wondered if anyone, when she left, would ever ask where she had been.

Richard had kept a hard face through the burial, and even when the sun came out he didn't soften, he didn't seem to notice; he never once cried. Nicole suspected he had always been jealous of Andy—who was doing a man's work, after all, while Richard always seemed to be playing at it, a boy strutting around in his father's big shoes and tie.

It wasn't, she knew, that Richard disliked her, or even that his parents disliked her. They were devastated by Andy's death, of course, and that was part of it. But what it really came down to was that she was a *Lombardi* and he was a *Cook*. After college Andy had dismissed the Manhattan elite, moved to Pensacola to attend Officer Candidate School, and bought a closetful of white shoes and blue name badges that said A. COOK. He had met her there, on the deck of a beach bar, her hair blown up like a candelabra by the wind, and she was a Lombardi and he was a Cook, yes, but he was A. COOK now and that made a difference.

They had always been ashamed of her, her rough manners and simple, lower-end, department-store clothing. So after the funeral, unemployed and unable to hire a lawyer to argue her case, she had sent away for graduate school catalogues and eventually found her way to a man in Miami named Stefan, who ran a discreet, profitable service for high-end clients. It had lasted four years, long enough to earn double what she owed in student debt, and her experiences had left her broken but well-off—polished, reserved, with a closetful of beautiful clothes and the poise to wear them.

Still, it was hard for her to understand sometimes how it had come to that. She had been a daughter once; she had almost been a wife. She used to spend Sundays at church with her father, and then one day he was gone. One day Andy was painting the shutters, and the next he was a fatality of war. She just couldn't understand how it had happened that he had been inside that helicopter when he had, just a moment ago, it seemed, been kneeling next to a paint tray, an ordinary man doing an ordinary chore.

And now that she was finally able to afford an independent lifestyle—able to move forward, forge a new identity, finance her first trip alone overseas—she had run into Richard, and all he seemed to see in her was the girl she had left behind.

He had sent her a letter once—his only correspondence, a note jotted on an index card. *There was no scene, no tears,* it said, *just thought—the long private thought of somebody who has to alter a whole course of life.* She was almost offended by it at first. It seemed to imply she cared only about herself. She hurried to find the book he had quoted: *The Quiet American,* it was called, apparently rather famous. She learned the character had lost a lover; her name was Phuong, which means phoenix. She thought she understood then what Richard had meant—that others had risen from loss, and that they would too—so she took it as a gesture of communion between them, and tried to forgive him.

When her plane landed in Dublin, an Indian man in a suit met her at the baggage claim with a sign that said N. LOMBARDI in blue marker.

* * *

In the cab, leaving the airport, Nicole watched the landscape move past her window. She decided that she wouldn't tell Richard she had been here before, that she had stayed in the Shelbourne Hotel with a stout middle-aged Irishman who had ordered her champagne and lobster. That was several years ago, just after Andy was buried, but it seemed like a time many years earlier, before they'd even known each other.

She had decided she was going to talk to the reporter; she would announce this to Richard at dinner. She was going to tell the journalist all about Andy and that they were going to be married. She was going to explain to him how she had sent the wedding gifts back, and what it was like to bring all those gifts to the post office and have the stupid girl comment on the pretty packaging, saying, "Oh, cute, is this for a wedding?" When she told him these things, he would hate himself for trying to argue that Andy had not died as bravely as she believed, for insinuating that her sadness was somehow not as worthwhile as it might have been.

Her driver was not chatty like those she remembered from her last trip. He took her politely and unsociably across the Liffey, past the chains of Londis and Easons and the endless squatting gray row houses. The sun wouldn't set for another hour, and the sky was glutted with gray cauliflower clouds tinged pink by the lateness of the day. She remembered Dublin as a cold, glamorous place, fresh and old at the same time—girls in their school uniforms and Wellingtons, calling each other *love,* the tiny crammed bookstores, the delicious bread and chocolate; in Dublin, it was desirable to have "good *craic*" and be "a cute *hoor,*" which had amused her at the time.

Richard lived in a third-floor apartment just off Grafton Street, which was cluttered with flashy storefronts and university students banging happily on their guitars. It surprised Nicole to realize that he lived in the "hip" area of the city, a place Andy would have liked. She remembered thinking this same thing about Andy as her Irish client had led her down the street to their hotel.

She was wearing a yellow sundress and white pins in her hair, and she checked her makeup in the driver's mirror before she stepped out of the car. She steadied herself in front of Richard's door. She was nervous, the way she'd been on the night they'd met. She supposed she wanted him to think well of her still, although she couldn't figure why. That night, Andy's father had taken them to dinner at a restaurant in New York, where, as if to impress her with their fine palates or embarrass her for her lack of one, Richard and his father had ordered her the prix fixe menu of raw fish and quail, and when she asked for sweetbreads she discovered that they were neither sweet nor bread, and only the wine had kept them in her stomach until the evening was over.

But when she knocked at the address she had been given, it was not Richard but an Irishwoman who answered the door. She was very tall and very slim; she had green eyes and red hair piled on top of her head. She must have been only slightly older than Nicole, but she had the air of someone who was genuinely, casually sophisticated, someone who wore jeans and ballet flats when she shopped, her purse hanging on her elbow. Nicole felt herself shrink in front of her.

"You're in the right place, love, don't be confused. You're Richard's friend?" The woman looked away for a moment, out of politeness or regret, and Nicole thought, *She knows everything that's happened, then—as much as Richard does at least.*

"I do hope Richard mentioned me," the woman said, laughing, as she ushered Nicole inside, up two flights of stairs to the third floor, where Richard was huddled ridiculously over the stove in the massive white kitchen, wearing what she could only imagine was the Irishwoman's pink apron. He was pouring the contents of a pan into a bowl.

"Nicole!" He turned to her and grinned, pulling off the apron and handing her a glass of wine. Richard introduced the woman as Moira, his girlfriend, and put his arm around her waist. "She's been very kind, helping me cook," he said.

It struck Nicole that Richard was aging as Andy would have aged, that standing in front of her was the face Andy would have had if he had lived to thirty-five. It occurred to her suddenly that this moment could have been theirs, that Andy could have finished his service and they could have moved to Dublin, lived here in this shiny soap-white apartment together. But instead it was this beautiful stranger who was sitting comfortably on the edge of the counter—what should have been *Nicole's* counter—and it was this other woman whose life was happening here, in this place.

"There's more space here than I imagined from the street," Nicole murmured. It was the only thing she could think to say.

"Yes, it's grand, isn't it?" Moira said. Standing, she slipped on her shoes again. "Well, I'll leave you two." She surprised Nicole with a hug.

"You're not staying?"

"No, I've got to run off to my mother's tonight."

"Does she live around here?"

"Out in Rathmines. It's not far. It was grand to meet you, though. You're lovely, just like Richard described you. Perhaps I'll see you again."

When she left, Nicole went to the window to watch her go. "She's very beautiful," she told Richard as Moira hurried along the street. "Does she live here with you?"

"Yes, she does."

"I like her. I suppose you're going to marry her?"

From behind her, Richard laughed. "I was thinking of it."

It had started to rain, and she watched the umbrellas bloom open in the street. Then, just as Moira disappeared, Nicole suddenly saw Andy looking up at her from across the road. He was standing in front of the newsstand with his hands in his pockets, wearing the same coat Richard had been wearing earlier. He was not smiling, though, as he usually did; instead he seemed upset, and it worried her.

When she turned back to Richard, a bit unnerved, he was watching her too, smiling a little. "So you've grown up," he said, coming up to refill her glass.

She said, "I suppose," but she was feeling distant. She was already somewhat tipsy from the wine, and she was worried about Andy's expression.

"I noticed your jewelry. You must be quite successful now yourself."

She felt her face burning. "I have my graduate degree in communications," she said. "I work for an advertising agency."

"That's wonderful."

He was still staring at her. She couldn't quite read him, and it made her uncomfortable. She hurried to say something. "I'm going to speak with that writer, Richard," she blurted. "There's nothing you can say to convince me not to."

Richard shrugged, leaning back against the dining room wall. "That's all right." He seemed almost amused by her insistence.

"What?"

"I don't mind if you talk to him."

She looked at him suspiciously. "I thought you asked me here to convince me not to."

Richard shook his head and frowned. "I have to confess something," he said. "I followed you into the cathedral today."

She laughed nervously. "What are you talking about?"

"I was having lunch at the hotel you were staying in, and I saw you. At first I almost couldn't believe it was you. . . .you looked so different. And—I followed you. I don't know why. But I wanted to see you."

Her head was swimming. "I don't understand. Why didn't you *say* something?"

"I didn't really—know what to say." He paused. "I know you hate me. And you should, really." Seeming embarrassed, he turned to the table and began setting out the silverware for dinner. "What happened after the funeral, letting my parents take that money—I should have said something. But I was a coward."

She was furious; he still couldn't face her, even now. Standing across from him in his home as he bumbled with the table settings—worrying over such small things, like folding the napkins—it occurred to Nicole that the note Richard had sent her all those years ago may not have been a gesture of understanding or concession. It seemed more likely now that it was some kind of dismal apology—not just for the way he had treated her, but for his whole self. Perhaps Andy's death had shamed him even more than it had saddened him. Perhaps it was an apology for his white coffee cups, his polished dishes, his manicured nails. Andy had always been the bigger man of the two. And when he died, how could Richard go back to his tiny days without guilt? But that was all the life he knew. He shuffled from room to room, smoked a cigarette, took a lunch break.

"Look at me," she demanded. "At least look at me if you're trying to apologize."

The night had grown black and filmy with rain, and she was dizzy and irritated from the wine. She wanted to tell him about the man she had been with at the Shelbourne—whose name she couldn't even remember now—and the others, who had taken her to Los Angeles and Chicago and New York, just two blocks from Richard's old building. She wanted to tell him what she had become, say the word out loud to him, for the first time, because she had never been able to say it to anyone before, not even to herself, and because she wanted him to understand how terrible those experiences had been for her, and that it was partly his fault—even if it wasn't, even if it turned out to be her own fault in the end, something she might have done anyway.

But when Richard turned around, he did not look the same to her as he had before. It was odd—something about the shape of his face. . . it looked younger, thinner. It was as if something had changed in him, and it frightened her a little. Her voice caught in her throat.

"What is it?" he asked.

"You look so much—like Andy."

He shrugged. "Yes, I know."

"No." She was trembling. "Just now. You really looked like him for a minute."

He looked at her kindly and put his hand on her arm to steady her. She started to cry. "Come over here, come sit down." He led her over to the couch. "It's all right," he said. She was sobbing now.

He held her. When she didn't pull away he moved his hand, hesitantly and awkwardly, from her cheek down to her neck. She didn't say anything, only cried harder, and then he seemed to find his courage, the first she had ever known him to have, and he kissed her, gently at first, but then harder, pushing her back onto the arm of the couch.

She tried to imagine that Moira would return, imagined Moira crying out, coming at him and putting an end to this.

But before she kicked him away, as hard as she could, she paused. Because perhaps—Moira would do nothing. Perhaps Moira wouldn't even recognize the man on the couch, because it wouldn't be Richard at all. And only Nicole would understand that it was *him*, he had come back after all, and somehow it would have happened, somehow things would have righted themselves in the end—just as Andy had promised her, just as she had always imagined.

All the Ways We Say Goodbye

When you grow up in New Jersey, in the dim gray suburbs of New York, you grow up with the knowledge that one day you will have to leave. You don't think to be sorry about it, because that's how it is. After high school, if you don't want to go to Rutgers, and you aren't smart or lucky enough for Princeton, you will be sent out of state, where you still have a shot at a good school, or a swim team scholarship. Once you are out, you can go anywhere. But if you do, it will be very hard to come back, even though there are things you will miss—the malls, your old elementary school, and summers at the Jersey shore, the fudge whipped in huge vats and the birds wheeling over the boardwalk.

Some of your more ambitious boyfriends will eventually find jobs in Manhattan. You know you could always marry one of them and live a glamorous few years in the city, but you also know where that leads. When you have kids you will trade in your SoHo apartment for a condo in Hoboken, and eventually you will want a yard and you will buy a small house in Jersey City, and then a bigger one in Madison or Morris Plains, and you will end up just where you started—in some four-bedroom new-build just off the interstate, with nothing to look forward to but your book club and late-night TV, and all that beautiful gothic promise of the city just out of reach.

That's why you try to get as far away as you can while you are young.

Still, wherever you go after that, it will be hard to call anyplace home. When you grow up with the idea that there is always something better out there, you can never truly stop wondering what's waiting for you somewhere else.

✦ ✦ ✦

Your mother, when she was young, was able to get away, for a brief six years. She got onto the highway straight out of college, with two suitcases and a parakeet in a wire cage, and she drove. For a while, in the '70s, she worked as a nurse in Richmond, at the hospital where Patch Adams taught, until she returned for a summer to her hometown of Pequannock, met your father, and never left again.

Still, when you are young, your mother's favorite bedtime stories are always the ones about Richmond. She tells you about the duplex she rented with the candy-pink walls, and the "Saturday Gun 'n' Knife Club," as she called it, that filled the hospital beds on Sunday mornings. She tells you about the young doctors she used to date, the ones who are married now, or divorced, or gone. She speaks about them as if there is still the hope that she can go back again, ten years later, and they will all be waiting for her.

From the time you are very young, you are aware that this part of her life—the part that's past—will always be the best part. Still, you see her as the kind of woman who has put her hands into the stomachs of dying men without thinking twice, the kind of woman who lived, and you love her.

You love your father too, but growing up you know very little about him, except that he is a good, quiet man who sells insurance in Newark and always comes home by 6 for dinner. You know that he collects Lionel trains and owns a small blue motorboat, which he keeps in the driveway and polishes when you have gone to bed; and you know that he loves the dog he bought when you were nine, a cocker spaniel named Marty, and that he spends his weekends on the wicker porch chair reading novels, with Marty balled up under his slippers like a stuffed toy. All of his novels are bought from old library sales and still have the catalogue card on the back of the front cover.

But you also know that your father grew up in Morris Plains, only three miles from where you were born, and that he has spent most of his life in this town. You know that his failed tryout as a varsity football kicker still troubles him, and that the stories he tells of his past are tedious, nothing like your mother's—just Saturday nights at the Dairy Queen and racing his Corvair down Route 287. He shows you the houses his friends used to live in when he was a boy, and for a long time you see him as a coward because he stayed, and because he fell in love with your mother and made her stay too, when she didn't belong in New Jersey anymore—it always seemed, when she looked at you, that she was wondering where she'd be if you hadn't come along.

*   *   *

It is not until you are nineteen, a freshman at Clemson in South Carolina, that you learn anything new about your father. By then your mother has been gone for six years—she joined the Army Nurse Corps at thirty-nine—and it is just you and your dad and Marty driving up to Lake George, New York, in May for your cousin's wedding. The cousin is on your mother's side, and the drive from New Jersey is five hours, what with the traffic, but your father still insists that you be there, that it is the right thing to do.

When your mother left for her first base in California, she promised to send for you when school let out. But then she fell in love with an army man and moved to Germany, and then you realized she would not be coming back. By the time of the wedding you have not spoken to her in over a year, and as far as you know no one else in the family has either. She could be anywhere in the world by then, in the Middle East or some hill town in Spain, having the adventures she always dreamed of when she was younger.

Your father takes Marty everywhere now that she's gone. You have always considered Marty his dog, not yours, and you are glad there is someone still at home to look out for your dad. You imagine the two of them sitting together on the porch under the shallow blue sky, like two old men who have been friends for a long time and have nothing left to say to each other.

On the way up your father asks you about your classes, and you tell him they are going fine and that you are thinking about majoring in English. He has never been the kind of father to ask you what the hell you are going to do with that; instead, he says he liked the stories you wrote for the literary magazine in high school.

When you ask him how he has been keeping busy, he says he has started exercising since he quit cigarettes; he takes Marty for long hikes on the weekends. When Marty hears his name, he pushes his pear-face into your shoulder from the back seat and waits for you to pat his head.

◆ ◆ ◆

The wedding is being held in a lodge overlooking the lake, a kind of campsite with a cluster of cabins around it. Before the ceremony you have some time to kill, and your father takes you into town to shop the outlets. He buys you a pair of dress shoes, and afterward you sit with him on a picnic table and look out at the blue lake, eating ice cream, your feet on the benches. The day is luminous, but the clouds are gorged with rain. "It'll come down soon," your father says, chewing his lip.

Then: "Let's take a trip," he says suddenly. You tell him you are already on a trip, and he says, "Just for an hour. I used to spend my summers as a boy just a little way from here."

You are surprised because, as far as you know, your father has never left New Jersey.

But then he takes you to the edge of town and keeps driving— north, into the woods—and he seems to know exactly where he's going. After a while there is no one else in sight, and the sun is gold on the trees, and you feel free and adventurous, as you imagine your mother felt once, driving south after college, with the windows open and her whole life waiting for her at the end of the road.

◆ ◆ ◆

He takes you and Marty through Warrensburg to a town called Pottersville, a battered nook in the woods of which there seems to be little left. At its edge there is a sign for a mining and tourist site called Stone Bridge and Caves, scraped almost white by the weather.

Pottersville is nothing like New Jersey, your father tells you. "My grandparents came out here from the city," he says, "because in the summers all the green space reminded them of Italy. There used to be raspberry bushes in the yard, and a drive-in theater out back. At night the lights from the projector would come through the trees. You could see them from our porch."

But now nothing of that remains. There is a 7-Eleven where the house used to be, and grass has grown up over the parking lot of the theater. You ask your father why he never told you about this place before, but he doesn't seem to hear you. He is leaning forward over the steering wheel, peering through the windshield, and you have never seen him look so sad before, not even when your mother left.

He says he wants to take you to visit your great-grandfather's grave, and you drive around for a bit, but you can't find the Catholic church, only a Lutheran one. You have to drive through the neighborhoods for ten minutes before you catch sight of someone outside, a man mowing his lawn, to ask him about the church.

But when you finally locate the graveyard, your father can't find the headstone. "I remember he was buried under a little tree," he says, but there are two dozen trees on the lot, and they might all have been little forty years ago. The graves seem to be grouped by ethnicity, and you follow your father from stone to stone, looking for the Italian names.

Marty sniffs around a little, and after a while you bundle him into your arms and say it's late, you should start heading back. He asks you for another ten minutes, but you're going to miss the ceremony, and when you tell him this his shoulders fall, and he stands there for a moment looking out over the sea of stones, stooped like an old man. Your father must have had so many stories, and not a day will go by after this that you won't think about them, and wish you had stayed another hour under the cool shade of the oaks.

Later, at the wedding, you get drunk because everyone keeps asking about your mom, and wondering if you have a boyfriend, and you dance with your father in the lodge, under a ceiling draped with tulle, to "Brown-Eyed Girl." Afterward, you don't remember much about that night, but you do remember your cousin and his bride kissing in the rain under a huge pink umbrella, and it is all so beautiful—her white dress, the misty colors of the evening—that you will remember thinking, I hope someone gets this photo, though you will never actually find out whether they do.

That night, your aunt knocks on your door and says you have to go to the hospital, your father has had a heart attack. She is still in the dress she was wearing at the wedding, a long gold evening gown, and she stands in the doorway with the moonlight burning her into a silhouette, so that she almost doesn't seem real, and you think,

Well, either she must be an angel or she must be a dream; because if she's not then she really is my aunt in her gold Macy's dress telling me my father has had a heart attack.

Far off, you imagine, in Pottersville, a row of brown, shingled houses filled with sleeping strangers, the children of the people your father used to know. And you feel like you have come to some kind of understanding in this place about the kind of man your father is, and that you have judged him meanly. You think that he is not a coward as you used to believe, but a man who was happy once. And you are the fool, because your father has called two places home in his lifetime, and when he goes, you will have none. And you think, what if all you do is wait for something better, something that never comes, and one day you take your own daughter to see what's left of Morris Plains, and it is just a sea of graves no one visits anymore.

◆ ◆ ◆

Your father is buried in New Jersey, in the plot he was supposed to share with your mother. Your mother does not come to the funeral because the only phone number you have for her belongs to a shrill German woman who thinks you are calling from some charity called the Kinderstern. Afterward you sell the house and bring Marty back with you to South Carolina, where you have rented a townhouse because you suddenly feel too old to be spending your nights in a dormitory, squealing over boys. You have to remember how to carry your nineteen-year-old body, how to mix a cocktail, how to laugh when your friend tells a joke about sex.

When you left New Jersey for college, you always knew there might come a time when you never returned again, but before, you always had a reason to go back if you wanted. All you have now is Marty, and he is with you, spending his afternoons lying solemnly in the middle of your kitchen floor. At first you aren't sure what to do with him; you never paid attention to how much he was fed or how often he needed to be walked. At night he cries until you carry him to the foot of your bed and arrange him on top of a towel with his stuffed aardvark.

Then one evening he crawls up while you are reading in bed and puts his head in your lap. It feels so natural that for a moment you can even imagine your dad in the room with you, sitting by the window with his feet propped up on a chair, reading one of his library novels and talking about the weather.

◆ ◆ ◆

After that, you live. You write papers and hold dinner parties and go to swim meets. Your aunt calls every once in a while to see how you're doing, and you tell her you're fine, you've started studying for the GRES so you can go for your doctorate after graduation. She asks you if you have talked to your mother. You say you tried to reach her, but you don't know where she's gone; there is someone else living in her old apartment now. This is only part of the truth. The other part is that every once in a while, in the early hours of the morning, you get a call from an unknown number. You always think about answering. You never do.

Then, in March of your senior year at Clemson, you find Marty splayed on the lawn near the deck. When the veterinarian sets his broken leg, he finds a tumor in Marty's throat. When he tells you this you can't stop thinking about your father, who died in the hospital twenty minutes before you arrived. All you can think is that Marty will die while you are at class or out buying groceries, and you will find him cold on your bed when you return. You don't want him to be afraid when it happens.

The vet tells you Marty will soon be in great pain and asks if you want to put him down. You do, but not here, not in this sterile, unfamiliar place, with posters of animal digestive systems on the walls. You tell him you'll think about it, and later you put Marty in your car and drive the ten hours north, through the night, to Pennsylvania, where your dad had a friend who works with horses. He owes you because one year at your parents' Christmas party, just after you turned fifteen, he stumbled into your pink-wallpapered bedroom and tried to kiss you, and you never told anyone.

When you explain what you'd like to do, he warns you against it, but in the end he gives you a needle and a bottle of sodium pentobarbital and shows you how to do it. I could lose my license for this, he keeps saying, but you take the bottle and leave before he changes his mind.

It takes another seven hours, all afternoon, to reach Pottersville. You pass Lake George on the way, and the lodge where your cousin was married. He is divorced already and seeing another girl. You remember the moment he had with his bride at the wedding, and you wish you had taken that photograph.

♦ ♦ ♦

You have to stop for gas just outside town, one of those old places where you have to pay inside. The man at the counter sees your license plate and asks what brought you all the way to a place like this. You tell him your father lived here once, before you were born; he used to tell you about it when you were little.

"Well, there's not much left now, but there's a neat place called Stone Bridge and Caves," the man says. "That's where I take my nephews when they visit." You stand there while he draws you an elaborate map on the back of your receipt. Outside, Marty's face is pushed against the window of your car, and you wish you could take him home again, but you know it wouldn't do any good.

You have to carry Marty because of his cast, and by the time you find a comfortable spot in the woods near the river, the sun is going down. You've been up for almost thirty-eight hours by now and haven't even thought about where you'll stay the night. Marty is tired, and whimpering. Good boy, you say. Shhh, it's all right.

You lay him on top of the blanket and fill the syringe like your dad's friend showed you. By the time you find the vein in his foreleg you are shaking, almost uncontrollably. Marty can sense something is wrong, and he nudges your hand.

You realize that until now, you have never really been alone, because when your mother left you still had your father, and after your father, you had Marty. But when Marty goes, you will have to face up to it for the first time, all at once, and you're not sure if you can do that, even though Marty is facing a near future of constant pain, and you'll never be able to bring yourself to do this again.

Finally, as you are telling him what a good dog he is, what a good, good dog, you get control of yourself and push the syringe into his leg. He moans, and when you realize what you've done, you feel sick and you take his head in your arms. You were told it would take up to twelve seconds, but fifteen pass, then twenty, and now the only thing you can think is that the son of a bitch filled the bottle with something else instead.

For a moment you don't want to believe it. Then Marty licks your hand, and you start to cry—furious, breathless sobs. You want to drive back and kill that man, who never even came to your father's funeral. You wonder where your dad is now and who, if anyone, was waiting for him when he got there. You know he was never good with new places, and must have been afraid at first. And you imagine bringing Marty back to that high steel table in the vet's office, with its lilac soap smell and its view of the recycling center out the side window, but you know he doesn't belong in that place; he belongs here, where your father had the kind of happiness that wasn't tainted by anything—not your mother's leaving, or your leaving, or his growing old alone.

Maybe it is a cruel thing to do. But you are in a bad state now, and all you can think is to take off your shorts and your tank top and bring Marty over to the river. You hug him to your chest, clutching him by the collar, and wade into the water until you are both fully submerged. You hold your breath, and he struggles, tearing at your shirt with his claws, but his desperate, choked noises are muffled, already faraway. And by the time you come up for air he is still, and it is done, and the black night is silvered with the eyes of the dead, looking down on you.

The View from Bonnell Lane

Until I was thirteen, I lived at the top of a steep hill called Bonnell Lane in Fairview, New Jersey, twenty minutes outside Manhattan. You could see everything from up there—people going in and out of little dolls' houses and taking their little matchbox cars in and out of driveways, and, in the distance, the skyscrapers. All day the airplanes went in and out of the city.

Now everyone who used to live on Bonnell Lane is gone, and builders have moved in and torn down the old houses and rebuilt them. It's hard to imagine the street as it was then, lined with boxy, brick-front houses, the yards patchworked with dirt and cheap red and yellow flowers. Back then, it was the place where people came to sled and to look at the city lights from the height of all the hills.

When I was ten my mother discovered I was nearsighted, and I began wearing thick pink glasses. About this time I'd graduated to middle school, where I made friends with a girl named Charlotte Lake. Charlotte had recently moved from California into a house at the end of Bonnell Lane, and because her last name began with the same letter as mine, she was assigned to sit behind me in the five classes we shared. I envied her for her perfect vision and her beautiful name. The daughter of a Hollywood cameraman, she had grown up near the ocean.

"There was a little cat," she told me once, "who lived on the beach near my house. I tried to bring her inside once, but she liked sleeping in the sand more than in a bed."

"What happened to her when you left?" I asked.

"I don't know."

"Maybe you can go back and find her when you're old enough."

Charlotte shook her head. "No. I don't think she'll be there anymore."

Charlotte lived on the side of the street where the houses sat a good twenty feet above the road, their driveways stretching precariously upward, their steep front lawns impossible to landscape. I lived on the opposite side, in a house that, tucked below street level, received much less sunlight than the houses across the way. I imagined that because Charlotte's parents had bought a house on the light-filled side of the street they must be worldly, sophisticated people. But when she invited me inside for the first time, I was surprised to see her mother curled up in her pajamas on the couch in the middle of the afternoon, watching Ricki Lake on TV. She turned her head when we came in but didn't get up. She was a large woman, her thick white ankles protruding from her sweatpants. Charlotte leaned over her and gave her an upside-down kiss on the cheek, while I stood behind them with my hands clasped in front of my waist.

Charlotte motioned me into the kitchen, where we sorted cookies and gummy bears into two bowls. Outside, we lay the bowls and a pair of bath towels at the top of the driveway and looked out over the whole of the neighborhood.

"Sorry about my mom," Charlotte said.

"What for?"

"When I went to your house your mom made us a snack and talked to us about school."

"Oh," I said. "She's only home then because she works in a restaurant. She's gone almost every night."

Charlotte nodded. "My mom's depressed. We moved up here after my dad died because her sister lives nearby."

"Your dad's dead?" I asked incredulously. It was like discovering the end of something you believe in. I had imagined he worked in New York.

"It was an accident. He got pinned under a set piece, and then he got an infection in the hospital."

"Oh," I said, and then, after a pause, added, "I don't have a dad anymore either."

Charlotte looked up, surprised. "What happened to him?"

"He left," I said, and immediately wished I hadn't. Unlike Charlotte's, my own story didn't really have an end, just a gradual fading away.

"At least he might come back," she said. "It's better than him being dead."

"No," I said. "Because he won't come back, and that's worse." I didn't tell her how he had loved my mother but not me; how, the night he left, they had stood holding hands by the window, looking at the city; and how there was always a part of me that wondered, when I turned eighteen and left, whether he might come back to her. As a child I remembered him reaching out to me hesitantly, like art, like something he would never quite understand enough to want.

We sat for a while listening to the airplanes, smacking gummy bears between our teeth. Charlotte picked around the bowl for the green bears. "Herr Haas lives on our street, you know," she said after a while.

"No way." I considered her skeptically. "I've lived here my whole life and I've never seen him."

Charlotte nodded. "He does. I see him driving past here every afternoon. He lives in the brick house on the corner." She pointed to the place where the street curved upward and out of sight. "You probably just never noticed him."

"Which house?"

"You can't see it from here. It's the one with the green door."

"How do you know which one it is if you can't see it from here?" I asked.

She shrugged.

"You *followed* him?"

She shrugged again. "What else am I supposed to do all afternoon? Sit inside and watch Maury Povich?" She shuddered. "It creeps me out, though, him being right around the corner like that."

Herr Haas had been teaching German for as long as anyone could remember. He was unmarried, somewhere past fifty but distinguished, the strands of his dark, oiled hair parted at the side. Half the girls were in love with him; the other half were afraid of him. We were obsessed, at the time, with the stars of our parents' generation, and the ones in love with him said he looked like an older Andrew Keegan. The others swore he stared at them when they weren't looking. But to me he always looked tired and a little lonely.

As sixth graders we were required to take a quarter each of German,

Spanish, and French, but my heart lay with Latin, and I think Herr Haas always sensed this betrayal in me. The Catholic churches were modernizing, but I had once been enchanted by a visit to a dark, moonlit cathedral in New York, the altar fogged with candle smoke. The priest clutched his gilded book and said the Mass in deep, sonorous tones, the choir sang "Ave Maria," and the nuns lifted their eyes to the ceiling to look at something I couldn't see.

On the first day of class, Herr Haas told us how as a newborn he had narrowly escaped the concentration camps in Dachau, how his mother had made a little pouch for him under her dress and fled across the border, pretending she was still pregnant.

A skater named Ryan Valentino asked, "How did you know not to cry?" and Herr Hass looked at him sharply and said, "All babies cry."

Ryan shook his head. "But then how—"

"My mother gave me whisky," he said, "and stuffed my mouth with a rag." He set his jaw. "This is what people did back then to save their families."

Everyone was quiet. We watched Herr Haas walk the aisles of the classroom, pulling at the stubble on his chin and inspecting us one by one. When he passed us, we held our breaths. He peered into the faces of everyone in the first row, and then the second, and when he came to my desk, he stopped. I was wearing a little wooden cross around my neck, and when he saw it he followed the chain up to my face and frowned.

At home, I told my mother I thought my German teacher disliked me because I was Catholic. She said that was ridiculous, and besides, priests had died in concentration camps too, but if it became a problem she would talk to the principal.

But I was uneasy. There were whispers that he still lived with his mother, whispers too that he may have once actually seduced a girl our age at a time when schools could still merely issue a reprimand and act like nothing had happened. What troubled us was the idea that we could spend an hour every day with a person whose life was completely unknown to us; though we did this every day with the others teachers, in Herr Haas's class it seemed there was something at stake somehow.

One of Herr Haas's greatest opponents was Ryan Valentino, who didn't understand our fascination with him, and after class Charlotte dragged me over to his locker in the hallway. He was eating potato chips out of a plastic bag and flipping through his notebook.

"Hey," Charlotte said, and Ryan Valentino closed his locker and turned around, looking at us with his pool-blue eyes.

"What's up?" He thrust out his chin in greeting and offered us each a potato chip.

Charlotte's eyes were shining. "I have something to tell you." She paused. "Herr Hass lives on Katie's and my street."

Ryan laughed and shook his head, and Charlotte nudged me. "He does, right? We can almost see his house from my house."

"He does," I said softly. "Right up the street."

Ryan looked at us with suspicion. "Seriously?" We nodded, and then he laughed. "You've *got* to do something about this."

"Yeah," Charlotte said, laughing too. "I know that."

"You should, like, spy on him or something. See if he really lives with his mom."

"But what if he does?" I asked. "Then what?"

"We'll see." He thought about it. "Bring a camera, though. See if you can get pictures of something embarrassing."

"Something like what?" I asked.

Ryan and Charlotte looked at me, annoyed. "Seriously?" Ryan said. "You *know* what I mean."

"Oh, that," I said, although I didn't know.

◆ ◆ ◆

After school we walked home together, and Charlotte was quiet. When I asked her what was wrong she said, "You don't have a crush on him, do you?"

"On who?"

"Ryan."

"Oh—no! No way." I tried to picture making out with Ryan Valentino, but I'd never made out with anyone before and the idea of starting with Ryan, who'd been in basements and closets with plenty of girls, made me uneasy.

"I think he kind of likes me."

I looked at her. "We're not really going over to Herr Haas's house, are we, though? Just because Ryan said to?"

She stopped and put her hands on her hips. "You're not *bailing* on me, are you? You're the one with the camera!"

"But your dad was a *cameraman*."

Charlotte glared at me. "Yeah, like, video cameras, and they belonged to the studio." Her face darkened. "And my mom got rid of most of his stuff when he died because she couldn't look at it anymore."

I loved the streets at this time of day, when ordinariness was something enviable. The retired couples walked their dogs and the mothers stood together on street corners waiting for their kids to get off the buses; it was still warm and the leaves fell onto the sidewalks and everything was as it should be. I knew my own mom would be standing at the sink by the kitchen window when I got home, and I felt sorry for Charlotte, who would never come home to see her mother in a window.

She looked at me suspiciously. "Why don't you want to do this thing with Herr Haas anyway? You're the one who said he was weird to you in German class."

"Not weird, really. He just looked at me funny."

"Because you're Catholic, you mean, or because you're a girl?"

"I don't know why," I said, although it was true that in three weeks of class he had never called on me once.

"So he's either a perv or he's got something against Catholic chicks. Either way that's weird."

"What religion are you?" I asked her.

"Protestant, I guess." She shrugged. "No one ever hates the Protestants. They're, like, friends with everyone."

"Yeah," I said, but I didn't tell her about the Mass in New York and everything she was missing.

"Let's meet up tonight," she said.

"I can't tonight. My mom'll be home."

"Tomorrow then. After dark." It was only September and the sun still stayed out till after 8. I hesitated.

"Please?" Charlotte bit her lip. "You're my only friend here."

We had reached my house and we stopped at the top of the drive-way. "Why don't you invite Ryan to go with you?"

She lit up. "Really?"

I nodded.

"You'd still have to come, though."

"Why?"

"Because I can't invite *just* him."

I sighed. "Fine." When I looked down at my house, I saw my mom waving from the kitchen in her red button-down waitress shirt.

◆ ◆ ◆

We met at Charlotte's house the next night just as the sun was going down. There was no moon, but the city was full of a thousand lights.

Charlotte was standing out front, wrapped in a gray sweater, her arms around her shoulders. "Ryan's not here," she said, stricken. I looked around, like he might appear at any moment, and she grabbed my hand. "Tell me you at least brought the camera?"

I shook my head. "I couldn't find it."

"How are we gonna do this without a camera?" She looked like she was about to cry. "How'll we show Ryan if we find anything?"

"We can go another night," I said. "We might not see anything anyway."

She looked back at her house; the TV was flickering blue in the living room window. "No," she said. "Let's still go."

We waited for Ryan, but he didn't come. Finally Charlotte looked up the street and sighed. "Okay," she said. We started up the side-walk; the lawns were empty, and there was no one in sight but a dog sniffing around in a side yard pen. There was a stillness to the night that seemed unnatural for late summer, and the moon was huge and swollen, tinged with red.

"Are you nervous?" Charlotte asked.

"I'm all right," I lied.

"What do you think he'll do if he catches us?"

"Nothing. I don't think he'll see us."

When we passed my house, the rooms were dark; my mom had gone to work and there wasn't anything to go back to. I felt a pang of longing for the first nights after my dad left, when we would sit in the dining room under the glittering chandelier, playing cards and waiting for him to come home. Back then, I still thought I could make it right with him if he did.

Herr Haas's house was eight houses past mine on the same side of the street. There were four or five windows lit downstairs and one upstairs. The house was only about half the size of mine and a third the size of Charlotte's, but someone had installed a pristine brick walkway from the driveway to the front door, and planted flowers all around it.

Charlotte was giddy. "It's *pretty*," she giggled. "Do you really think he *gardens?*" We raced down the driveway into the backyard, where no one could see us from the road, and huddled together in the bushes beneath a first-floor window. "I don't want to look," she said. "What if he's got something really weird going on in there?" She took a piece of gum out of her pocket and popped it into her mouth, chewing furiously.

"I'll look," I said. I pulled myself up to the windowsill and peered inside.

Herr Haas was sitting on a sofa in the living room, watching TV in a pair of green flannel pajamas. Next to him was a small, pink-slippered woman with white hair, probably his mother, reclining on a chair with a pile of sewing in her lap. She was so tiny it was hard to imagine her as a woman who had braved the worst parts of a war.

Then Charlotte looked too, and she grabbed my arm. "He does—he lives with his mom! He looks funny in those pajamas," she said.

Herr Haas said something and then got up and went into another room.

"Where's he going?" Charlotte asked.

"I dunno." We crouched there, watching his mother move her needle slowly back and forth. She worked with a fluid, soothing motion, and I could almost understand why Herr Haas still lived with her. It was something to rely on, this tiny woman in her chair every night, sewing her pictures.

Then, suddenly, we heard a soft noise behind us. Someone was on the lawn, coming around the side of the house. I froze. Charlotte choked on her gum, and I spun around—and there was Ryan

Valentino standing over us, hunchbacked, trying to shield his body behind a bush. When Charlotte saw him, she couldn't stop coughing. He put his hand over her mouth and then rapped her on the back until she spit her gum into his palm.

"Holy crap," she said, breathless. "You *scared* me."

Ryan grinned, tossing the wad of gum into the dirt. "You girls scare like chicks."

"We *are* chicks," Charlotte countered, but she was beaming. "You made it," she said.

"You kidding? This is *crazy* cool. I can't believe we're here."

"You were right, by the way," Charlotte said. "It's his mother in there with him."

"Oh yeah?"

We turned back to the window, and Herr Haas was in the room again, on the sofa. He sat there for a while watching the news. Every once in a while he would turn and say something to his mother, and she would nod or smile and say something back. After a few minutes, Ryan frowned. "This is kinda boring."

Charlotte went pale. "Something could still happen."

"I dunno."

I looked at my watch and thought of my grandparents in Florida. "It's 9:15. They probably just watch TV and go to bed at 10."

"But we can't see into his bedroom," Ryan said, "where all the good secret stuff happens. Why didn't you guys tell me his house was *two* stories?"

Charlotte panicked and then thought of something. "You and I could go for a walk and then come back," she said.

Ryan knew what she was saying. He ran his fingers through his black hair. "Yeah. That would be cool, I guess."

But then, all of a sudden, Herr Haas turned sharply toward the window and stood up. We all threw ourselves onto the ground, pressing our bodies as close to the side of the house as possible. I was almost on top of Ryan, and I could smell his sweat and shampoo. His shirt was covered with dirt, and he seemed whole and real, like part of the earth.

"Oh my God, oh my God," Charlotte breathed. "He can't see us, can he? I mean, you can't see outside at night, right, if there are no lights?" We could almost feel Herr Haas standing at the window above us, peering out into the dark, but we were too afraid to look up.

Ryan put his arm around Charlotte. "Just lay here for a second—then we run."

My heart was pounding. "No, you guys. This is crazy. I'm going home."

Charlotte grabbed my arm. "Don't! He's gonna *see* you if you go now!"

But already I had pulled away, and I was tiptoeing around the house toward the front yard. I could see the streetlamp fifty feet in front of me like a beacon, marking the sidewalk. All I had to do was sprint, and I would make it.

"Hey!" I turned around to see Herr Haas standing at the front door, less than ten feet away from me. He was just a shadow against the bright light of the hallway. "What do you think you're doing creeping around here?"

I couldn't bring myself to run. I looked up at him and then back at the street.

Herr Haas took a step forward, and I could see him clearly now, squinting into the dark. "*Katherine?*" he called.

I shook my head, as if to convince him it wasn't me, only someone who looked like me.

"What are you doing here?"

I could only think of one thing. "I—I live down the street."

"But what are you doing in my yard?"

"I don't know." I looked at the ground. "Taking a walk. I'm sorry."

He stared at me, pulling on his chin. Finally he said, "Do you want to come inside?"

I wasn't sure if it was a question or an order. I pictured Charlotte in the backyard, clapping her hand to her mouth and trying not to yell to me to run. But I couldn't run anyway. We had watched him, and now he was watching me; I thought about my mother, closing herself into her room alone every night, and about where she might be at that very moment if I hadn't come along.

And now Herr Haas was calling me, and I had to go. It was my time. I shuffled toward him down the walkway, and he stood back and held the door open for me. "I'm sorry, I'm sorry," I whispered as I passed him, so closely that for a moment I could smell his damp hair.

He ushered me into the kitchen. It was clean and white. "Just wait here a minute," he said. I glanced out the window but couldn't see Charlotte or Ryan, although I knew they were there. Herr Haas went into the living room and I watched him help his mother out of her chair. She was shaking a little and I could see what Ryan and Charlotte and I had missed before, that she had an IV in her arm, running to a plastic bag next to the chair. He helped her into a downstairs bedroom and after a few minutes he came out, shutting the bedroom door behind him. We were alone.

"Would you like a drink?" he asked, opening the refrigerator. "I've got Diet Coke, Sprite, or orange juice."

"Sprite, thank you." My mouth was dry. As he was pouring it I coughed and tried to think of something to say. "I live down the street," I said again.

"Does your mom know you're taking walks this late at night?"

"My mom's at work."

"I see." He set the drinks on the table and then sat down across from me, pressing his lips together. His hair, always perfectly combed in class, was tangled. Even with the small table between us, I could smell the mint of toothpaste on his breath. "What are you really doing here?" he asked finally.

I looked away. "Nothing—I don't know."

He nodded. "Katherine," he said slowly. "Let me ask you something."

"Okay," I whispered.

"What do the kids at school say about me?"

I looked down at the bubbles in my glass, sizzling to the surface. "They don't say anything."

He put his hand on the table next to my hand. "It's all right. I know they do." I felt dizzy. I tried to fix my gaze on something in the room but my eyes kept going back to the window, which was black as space. But then he took his hand away and said, hesitantly, almost like a question: "They laugh at me."

It wasn't what I had expected at all. I looked at him and saw he was still in his green pajamas, and I felt like I was trespassing on something sacred. Teachers were supposed to come to school at 7 and leave at 4 and come back again at 7 the next day. No one was supposed to know where they went or what they did when they left; they weren't supposed to have other, non-school lives, and they weren't supposed to invite students inside and show them where they ate and watched TV and put their mothers to bed.

"Only—some of them," I said finally. "Not all of them."

"Why?"

I looked at my hands. "I don't know. There are rumors. . . that you live with your mother, I guess, is one of them."

"Oh." He closed his eyes and leaned back in his chair.

"You don't have a German accent when you speak in English," I said, trying to change the subject, and he opened his eyes again.

"I've lived here almost my whole life. I went to your middle school, actually, when I was your age."

I looked at him. "You did?"

"It was different then. There were only twenty people in my grade."

"What happened to them all?" I asked, as if maybe they were still hanging around somewhere.

"Oh, different things. Most of them went to work in the city. Some went to war and never came back. One of them I married."

"You were married?" I tried to imagine marrying someone I already knew, like Ryan Valentino, and after the wedding going back to my mom's house and my bedroom with its purple wallpaper, and I wondered if that was how the rumor about him and the student got started, manipulated until it became something terrible.

"She left after. . . well, a few years into it. She couldn't stand it here after a while, everything changing but her staying the same, doing the same things she'd done when she was a kid."

"My dad left too," I said, "but I don't really know why." After a second I added, "He and my mom really loved each other."

He nodded. "I see."

I took a breath. "Herr Haas—"

"You don't have to call me that. You can call me Charlie."

Inside, my chest felt like a thunderstorm. "In class. . . you never call on me."

"Oh," he said. He let out a long, heavy breath, and when he was finished his shoulders were hunched and he looked deflated.

I shook my head. "It's okay. It doesn't matter. I should go." I was afraid he would think I had invited something, and I wasn't even sure that I hadn't.

He frowned, running his hand across his head to straighten the few strands of hair. Then he stood up and went into the living room and I thought that was his signal that it was time for me to go, so I stood up too. But when he came back he was holding something in his hand, a picture in a tiny silver frame. "I had a daughter once," he said slowly, holding it out. The picture was of a girl a few years younger than me, with green eyes and a tiny sliver of space between her front teeth. I stared at her. Except for her age and the age of the photograph, we could have been sisters.

"When I saw you," he said, so softly I could barely hear him, "at first, I thought it was her."

"What—what happened to her?"

He shook his head. "She died when she was ten. That was over twenty years ago, of course."

"I'm sorry." He had lived a whole life already, I saw, but it had only brought him back to where he had started. Having a brief happy life suddenly seemed worse to me than having a long sad one.

"There was a fire at her friend's house. It was nobody's fault," he said, as if he had been reassuring himself of this all those years. "But my wife left after that."

All of a sudden I saw, clear as day, that there was everything different about us and everything the same. I thought about the nuns in New York and all the wonderful things they must have known that none of the rest of us knew, things that kept them happy even though they could never get married or have children or go swimming. I asked him, "Have you tried praying for her?"

Herr Haas waved his hand in the air. "Oh," he said, as if prayer was something only children believed in. "I don't think so."

I reached out and put my hand on his arm. "It doesn't make them come back. It's just so you know they're okay."

He patted my hand, but he was already far away, with the people he used to know.

"You know, my mom'll be home soon," I said. "I should get going."

"Yes, yes." He cleared his throat and stood up. "You can stop by and say hi if you're ever up this way again," he said, and I said okay, although I wasn't sure I ever would. He led me back into the hallway and out the door, and then I was back in the hot spring night again.

Charlotte and Ryan were waiting for me on the neighbor's lawn. "Oh. My. God!" Charlotte jumped up when she saw me. "You were in there forever. What *happened* in there?"

"Nothing, really."

"Did he try to touch you?" Ryan asked.

I shook my head, and Charlotte sat down next to me and gripped my hand. "What was it *like* in there? What did he do?"

I shook my head. "It was just, like—I don't know, a regular house. Weren't you guys watching?"

"We got scared and ran off when he caught you. Did you meet his mom?"

"She went to sleep when I got there."

Charlotte's eyes were wide. "So you were alone with Herr Haas all that time?"

"Katie," Ryan said, putting his hand on his forehead, "that was *crazy!* This was, like, the craziest night."

Next to me, Charlotte beamed.

"You know, he's not that weird, you guys," I said. "He's nice."

Charlotte looked betrayed. "Katie—he's *creepy!*" She turned away. "I don't understand you at all."

After a minute I stood up and we walked home in silence. Ryan broke away first, at the corner of Bonnell and Ash, and then Charlotte and I parted.

◆ ◆ ◆

After that Charlotte and Ryan were a couple, and she started taking the bus home with him after school. A week later, my mom lost her job at the restaurant and decided she couldn't take another winter shoveling that steep driveway. She put the house on the market and took us to live with my grandparents in Cape Canaveral, Florida, where she'd grown up. She said she wanted to get her bachelor's degree. She was young still, only thirty-two. She said it could be—other than having me—like the last thirteen years hadn't really happened. She asked me if that was okay, if I knew what she meant, and I said yes, that what I really wanted, more than anything, was just for her to have a long, happy life.

When the movers came I knew we would never see my father again. I took one last walk down Bonnell Lane and saw Charlotte watching the trucks from her bedroom window. She waved, and I waved back, and that was the last time I saw her.

I wrote a letter to Herr Haas on a piece of the thick cotton paper my mother had bought for her college applications. The paper came in a cardboard box, not in plastic wrap, and at the top of the page I wrote, *I am writing to you on the nicest paper I have ever used.* I told him that I wouldn't be in his class anymore, but that I would think of him from time to time in Florida. And maybe one day if I came back and he was still living at number 32, I would stop and say hello; but if I never did, I hoped he would find what he was looking for.

I folded the letter and took it to his house. In his mailbox there was already a stack of envelopes, and underneath them, a thick blue book. When I pushed aside the letters I saw that it was a Bible—one of those free hotel Bibles you can request by mail. Sometimes we'd find Bibles like that in our mailbox, sent for no reason at all except that my mother's name had ended up on a list. But still, it seemed like something important had occurred, and in the face of it the letter I had written suddenly said nothing at all.

♦ ♦ ♦

When we got to Cape Canaveral I swam every day in my grandparents' pool. My mother went to the community college to become a nurse, and I learned that they didn't do that many rocket launches anymore. Instead, everyone talked about what it had been like forty years before, in the '50s and '60s, when you could run into people like Neil Armstrong and Alan Shepherd in the grocery store.

Then I always thought about Herr Haas, sitting behind a desk at Fairview School, flirting with the girl who would become his wife. That Herr Haas didn't know yet that this girl would leave him, or that one day he would watch his daughter go into a house she would never come out of again. This was the Herr Haas I liked to think about—the one who didn't know a girl named Katie Barrett, had never invited her into his home for Sprite or told her class stories about Germany during the war. In this Herr Haas's life, Katie Barrett might never know the color of his kitchen, might never see his mother, a woman had once fled Dachau in a dazzling act of bravery, reduced to a small woman in pink slippers. She might never know anything about him, because this Herr Haas still had a chance to become a man who wrote novels and rode elephants; he still had a chance to marry a woman who wouldn't leave and father a daughter who wouldn't die and never know of people like Katie Barrett or Ryan Valentino or Charlotte Lake.

And it would be okay with Katie Barrett if, somehow, she went back to Bonnell Lane again and there had never been a Herr Haas living in the house with the green door. That would be alright with her.

A Home Like Someone Else's Home

Once she'd dreamed of skyscrapers, street noise, and late nights in steaming diners, but she ended up instead in the brown, flat prairie on Highway 32, driving to a prison in Shelton, Iowa. It was a tiny, postage-stamp town, the kind people pass through on their way to someplace else. But every once in a while, there are one or two who don't make it to the other side, and Bobby Kovacev was one of those. She drove to visit him with a pretty, black-haired girl called Yasmina in the passenger seat, and Irene didn't know Yasmina very well, or Bobby at all. But all three of them had somehow ended up here.

He was just a name on paper then, a middle-aged man arrested for threatening his wife, and then a Bosnian man detained for illegal immigration. Yasmina was Bosnian-born as well; she and Irene both worked for a law office in Iowa City, though neither of them were lawyers. Yasmina was a translator, Irene a researcher. Other than that, they had nothing in common except that they were both driving to Shelton, Iowa to see Bobby Kovacev in his prison cell.

◆ ◆ ◆

The men's jail was small, just two stories tall. It could have been a schoolhouse except for the barbed wire on the fence around the basketball courts. Across the street was the shell of a train station with wide white boards over its doors. Irene and Yasmina stopped at a pizzeria for lunch, and it was crowded with all the women and children waiting for visiting hours.

Squeezed into a corner table, Yasmina leaned forward. "We have to say we're his lawyers," she said, "or they won't let us see him privately."

"Will that work?" Irene asked, skeptical.

"I'm twenty-five. Twenty-five is when people graduate from law school." She spoke nearly perfect English. She enunciated every word with her tongue against her white teeth.

"What do you know about him?" Irene asked. All she knew was that his first name was actually Bojan, but he had asked to be called something more American.

"Nothing except that he is married and he has been in detention for forty days." She held up her hands. "Who knows what else? He can't understand a word they are saying to him."

"Forty days isn't very long."

Yasmina frowned. Irene had learned two things during her three weeks at the law office. The first was that immigrants could be detained for years before they were either released or deported; the second was that in six years, her firm had managed to secure the release of only five people. What they really did was try to make them comfortable for the long haul; mostly they dealt with shaving cream, phone cards, and hills of paperwork.

Yasmina blotted the oil from her pizza onto a napkin. "I am worried that we have only an hour. Bosnians—if you ask them one thing, they talk forever. Because I am younger, it is rude for me to interrupt him."

Irene laughed. "But you can't think about him like an uncle or something. It's a detention center, not Bosnia."

"Your father," Yasmina said, changing the subject. "He is living with you?"

Irene's father had arrived a week earlier, bundled in a sweater even in the heat. In the doorway, he fumbled with a stuffed bear and a handful of balloons, the ribbons caught on the hallway lights.

She had rented a one-bedroom apartment in a building on fraternity row, where next door, college students doomed to summer school lounged on the front porch with beer bottles in their hands. The building was tired from so many winters, the floors sloping like the backs of old men and black dust packed into the crevices of the window frames.

No one, since she'd arrived in Iowa, had asked her about the mass of scars on the left side of her face, which was rude because until they asked it would be all they thought about. Eventually she told some of them anyway, about the fire in her college dorm, and the masks of gauze, and about having to have her yearbook picture taken not face forward but with her looking over her shoulder at the camera, as if it were someone she was saying goodbye to. What she didn't tell them was that two weeks before the fire, she'd won a modeling contest sponsored by a women's magazine and had been scheduled to meet with the editors in New York that summer.

"You are lucky," Yasmina said, dabbing her face with her napkin, "that your family is here."

Irene shook her head. "Not really. My mother died a year ago from cancer." Her father had arrived in Iowa with a stunned look on his face, as if his wife had just passed away the day before. It had suddenly hit him that she was gone.

Yasmina hesitated. "My mother is in Germany with my sister. They are waiting for my father there."

"Where is he?"

"Croatia, maybe."

"Why Croatia?"

"This is the last place we saw him when we left Bosnia during the war."

"But the war was—that was years ago—"

"Yes."

"Oh." Irene paused. "So why aren't you in Germany with them?"

Yasmina shrugged. "They could come here as refugees, like me. My mother is Muslim and my father is Christian. That makes it dangerous in Bosnia for us. But they won't come without my father." She thought about it. "And. . .I have a boyfriend here now. He has a three-year-old daughter. She doesn't have a mother. I guess I am kind of like her mother."

After her college graduation, Irene's father had retired and followed her to Iowa, where a college professor had found her a job. Her father slept on a couch in the living room, and spent his first few days wandering around the apartment looking for things to fix. He had never been retired before, and after a few days hanging around Dickson's hardware store he had gotten himself hired. Now he left for work the same time she did, and when she got home at night she sometimes found him leaning over the fence at the fraternity house, talking to a couple of the boys.

It was close to 12 o'clock. People in the restaurant were starting to get up and collect their belongings. A line was forming outside the women's restroom; makeup was extracted from sequined purses. By the time the line thinned, however, all the chattering had stopped. Slowly, silently, the procession of women filed across the road, bent under the hot sun. Just beyond the prison walls, fields and fields of open ground stretched in all directions like a cruel joke.

♦ ♦ ♦

A sign on the wall warned that visitors could not enter in strapless tank tops or short-shorts, and many of the women nervously shimmied their skirts a little lower past their hips. They had driven, perhaps, hours, and they were fearful it would be a wasted trip. Irene wondered if the visiting ever became a chore, and what it must feel like to want to abandon someone you love because of a long car ride.

In the corner by the desk where Yasmina waited to show their identification, a flag hung limply on a pole. Protect and serve, it said. On the far side of the room was a glass wall with a row of chairs and telephones; on the other side of the glass the men, talking to wives or girlfriends or children, looked only half real. It seemed possible that they could even be the ghosts of men, and one would never know, because it was impossible to touch them to see if they were warm. Life was on one side of the glass and on the other side there was something else that was not exactly life.

It was not like prisons she had heard about or seen in movies; maybe it was the heat, but the jail was as quiet as a library. Many of the men wore thick glasses and slicked-back hair; the young ones looked like scholars, like guys she would have flirted with in college. In fact the whole lobby reminded her of school: the clean, speckled tiles and the too-bright lights. There was a Coke machine in the corner, but not enough chairs. She didn't feel right taking a seat when the other younger women were settling themselves on the floor, but they were supposed to be lawyers, and after a moment of panic she decided lawyers would probably take the chairs. Keeping up this ruse was part of her job; she couldn't tell anyone the truth, which was that if an attorney drove eighty miles to feel out every case that came his way, he would be bankrupt in a month.

"This *heat*," a large woman beside her huffed, her hands clasped tightly in her lap. "Can't stand it." She looked at Irene. "You lawyer?"

Irene nodded.

"I'm here for my man." She narrowed her eyes. "He didn't do it though."

"Do what?"

"Whatever they say he do."

Irene didn't ask any more questions. It was a facility for detained immigrants, but a lot of the men had been discovered after committing other crimes.

Then an officer was standing over them with his arms crossed over his chest. "You can follow me," he said, and the other women turned spitefully to watch them go, not over to the chairs by the glass wall but through a door to the other side, where their husbands and boyfriends and sons lived and slept, dreaming about Chinese food and highways.

Their client was waiting for them in a room down the hall, wearing an orange T-shirt and a pair of gray sweatpants. He was seated behind a long wooden folding table, and Yasmina set her briefcase down across from him.

"Gospodin Kovacev." She reached over the table to shake his hand. "Dobro jutro."

Irene also reached forward. "Mr. Kovacev."

He pulled back and waved his hands at her. "Bobby, Bobby!"

"Bobby, I'm sorry. I'm Irene." She took the other open chair, which was set back against the wall, but didn't pull it up to the table.

He had a pale, round face, but it didn't seem like the face of a criminal. It was a gentle face, with three long lines across his forehead. He had made an effort to gel and comb his hair. She was reminded of her father during her mother's last mornings, when her mother would wake up lost and he would help her change her underwear and brush her teeth because those are the things people did in the mornings, although it all seemed like a terrible waste of time.

It struck Irene as odd that her father, in his last years in the air force in the early '90s, may have flown with his bombs over Bobby Kovacev's house in Bosnia. He remembered him saying to her once,

"If you kill someone, people celebrate you like you're a damn hero. But sometimes you are, and sometimes you aren't."

Yasmina was talking quickly now. She put her watch on the table and then leaned forward and crossed her ankles. For a moment her foot slipped out of her shoe and Irene caught a glimpse of a round, black imprint on her heel from the cheap shoe dye. She heard some English words amid the rush of Bosnian: *domestic assault* and *collect calls.*

When Bobby spoke, he was reserved at first, holding his palms flat together on the table as if he were praying. Yasmina sat back in her chair and listened. He had a slight lisp, and he spoke deliberately and rhythmically, emphasizing every other word, the way some of Irene's college professors had found themselves lapsing into meter.

Then, in the middle of their conversation, he stopped abruptly. He was fixated on Irene's face, and she knew he had just noticed her scars. She looked at her hands.

Suddenly Bobby's voice got louder. She looked up and saw he had taken his feet out of his sneakers and kicked them to the side. He stood up, and in the mirror behind him she could see Yasmina's wide, frightened eyes.

He began violently motioning with his hands. Something bad was happening. Yasmina tried to calm him down. "Sjesti," she kept saying, "Molim te, sjesti."

And then Bobby collapsed into his chair, throwing his hands over his eyes. One of the guards came into the room and put his hand on Bobby's elbow. "Come on now," he said. "Time's up."

Yasmina stood up. "But we have twenty minutes!"

"Time's up," the guard said again, and pulled Bobby out from behind the table.

Irene stood against the wall as they passed her. When they reached the door, Bobby stopped and turned around. "Miss Irene." His voice was pleading. His carefully combed hair had fallen over his face.

She looked at him, startled.

"You are—" He struggled to find the words. "You are like me." And then he hung his head, as if exhausted by this revelation, and disappeared into the hallway.

❖ ❖ ❖

"The attorneys will not take the case," Yasmina said when they left.

Irene shielded her eyes from the sun. "But—why not?"

"They will not win. He is schizophrenic."

Irene blinked. "How do you know that?"

"They showed me his file at the desk. This is how they caught him. He went to a doctor raving that voices were telling him to 'do something' about his wife. The doctor was afraid; he called the police."

"'Do something'?"

"That is what the file said."

"You mean—they arrested him because he was trying to get *help*?"

"Because they thought he was dangerous, and they found out he was illegal." She frowned. "If he is not legal, I suppose it does not matter why they arrested him."

"It isn't right."

She shrugged as if it didn't bother her but Irene could tell it did. "It does not matter. The lawyers will not win with him."

They were quiet as they drove back to the city. Irene watched as the little town of Shelton disappeared behind them. It was nearly 3 o'clock. Children were walking down Main Street wearing pink and blue backpacks.

"My boyfriend can pick me up at your house," Yasmina said. "We live outside of town. It is quite far."

"Are you sure? I don't mind driving you."

"No, it is all right."

After a while, Irene said, "But what *happened* in there exactly?"

Yasmina opened a window to let the air in. "When I asked about his wife he got upset. He said he would never hurt her. It was sad. He did not seem to understand that what he said about her is not why he is being kept there at all."

"Is that why he was crying?"

She hesitated. "He was in the Croat army," she said. "But his city is controlled by the Serbs now. He says they will kill him if he goes back there." She glanced at Irene. "What he said to you before we left—what was he talking about?"

Irene shook her head. "I don't know," she said, but many years later, she would still remember the moment when Bobby Kovacev had noticed her scars and said to her, *You are like me.*

❖ ❖ ❖

At Irene's place they found her father on a ladder next door, fixing the sign above the fraternity house door. The driveway was empty, and the brothers weren't hanging around. Irene burned with embarrassment. "Dad!" she called, getting out of the car. "Did they ask you to do that?"

He waved and made his way slowly to the ground. Irene put her hands on her head. "You *can't* just go around fixing other people's stuff."

"They're our neighbors."

"They're *my* neighbors." Irene turned to Yasmina. "Come on up. It's cooler inside."

Yasmina looked up sharply, as if she had forgotten Irene was there. "Oh," she said, "yes, thank you."

Inside the air-conditioner sputtered but ran. Irene took some glasses out of the cabinets as Yasmina looked around at the cardboard-box TV stand and bare floors.

Embarrassed, Irene said, "It's not much, but—" She almost said, *I don't know how long I'll be here.* But the job was the only one she had at the moment, and there really wasn't anyplace she was yearning to go.

"No, this is very nice."

Irene's father came in, wiping his forehead with a handkerchief. "I'm Charlie," he said, holding out his other hand.

"Yasmina. It is a pleasure to meet you."

"How did the interview go?"

"We will see, I suppose."

Irene set down the drinks. "So, I'll get to meet your boyfriend today."

"Yes. He is bringing his daughter also."

"Yasmina's family is in Germany, Dad."

Charlie nodded as if considering this. "Nice country now," he said finally. "My wife and I took a trip to Berlin once. There's a lot of excitement there, a lot of energy. Do you see them a lot, your family?"

She frowned. "Perhaps soon. It is quite a lot of money at the moment to travel."

"Those airlines are crooks. It cost me $500 to fly out here from Connecticut."

"Will you go back to Connecticut?"

He thought about it. "I'm not sure."

"Dad!" Irene stared at him.

Charlie held up his hands. "What would I do there, sitting in that big house all day?"

"I don't know—whatever you want. That's the point of retiring."

Yasmina smiled. "What did you do before you retired?"

"I was an engineer." He shrugged. "Spreadsheets and numbers."

Irene stood up too. "I'll be right back." She went through the bedroom into the bathroom and stood at the pedestal sink, listening to the low hum of their voices. She was angry with her father, but she didn't know why—because he was giving up the house her mother had died in? She wasn't sure what she wanted from him. She washed her face and forced herself to look in the mirror, at the pink, distorted skin that ran from her forehead to the left side of her chin, as if someone had tried to smooth crinkled wrapping paper over her face.

But at the same time, she remembered how in the moment of the fire she would have given everything to be standing, alive, in a bathroom in Iowa City looking at herself in the mirror.

When she went back into the bedroom the voices had stopped. She looked into the living room and saw Irene and her father standing at the apartment door. They didn't say anything. Yasmina closed her sad, black eyes and put her hand on his shoulder. And then, very gently, her father reached up and patted Yasmina's elbow.

This is what he had done for Irene in the hospital, when she was wrapped in gauze and the doctors said it was the only place he could touch her without pain. For weeks, he had sat by her bed patting her elbow and reading chapters of the Boxcar Children because she had loved the books when she was little.

"I have to go," Yasmina said. "My boyfriend is waiting downstairs."

"He can come upstairs if he'd like," Charlie said.

"Thank you. But we have to get home. And he has Sophie in the car seat."

"We'll walk out with you then."

Outside in the driveway, her boyfriend was leaning against the car. He was a good-looking guy, tall, with sandy hair and scruff under his chin. Yasmina stood on her toes and kissed him without lifting her arms from her sides.

The little yellow-haired girl in the backseat leaned forward and waved at Irene.

"Thank you for the drink," Yasmina said. "You have a lovely family." Irene looked at her dad. It hadn't occurred to her before that having one person was having a family.

She watched them turn the corner onto Clinton Street. At the light, the boyfriend reached behind him and tickled the little girl's stomach. In an alternate reality, Irene thought, that could have been her life. But then she remembered that without the fire, she would have been in New York, not Iowa. None of their lives had turned out like they'd thought. And the best any of them could do was to find a home that seemed, even if it wasn't theirs, like someone else's home.

Her father watched her as she stared after them. "We could go out to dinner," he said.

She bit her lip. "There's somewhere I have to go first." She ran inside for her purse and searched for the paper the law firm had given her with Bobby Kovacev's personal details: name, birth date, home address, prison address. He had lived in a country town called Ely not far from Iowa City.

She went downstairs and got in the car, but her father stood in the driveway. "Aren't you coming?" she asked him.

"Oh," he said. "I didn't know if you wanted me to."

"Of course I do."

He went around to the other side and got in. "Is this about that man you saw today?"

"Yeah." She wanted to talk to him about the change that had come over Yasmina after their visit. But she wasn't quite sure where to begin, or what she was even looking for in Ely.

"It'll be light out for a while," her father said meaninglessly, peering at the sky.

Iowa City was only fifteen minutes wide from one side to the other, and then they broke out into the country. They drove for twenty minutes down the same long road until a sign said *Ely* and Irene pulled into a gas station. A man came outside with a bucket of soapy water and a squeegee for her windshield.

"Do you know where Rowley Street is?" she asked him.

He pointed. "Just off Main," he said, "half a mile that direction." Every town in Iowa had a Main Street.

The town was all storefronts and brick and American flags, like Shelton. Bobby Kovacev's apartment was the top floor of a small house next to a laundromat. Charlie waited in the car while she went up to the porch and buzzed upstairs. When no one answered, she buzzed the first floor.

A woman came outside barefoot, in a cotton T-shirt and shorts, and Irene turned a little to the left so the woman could only see the good side of her face. "I'm sorry to bother you, but I'm looking for Mrs. Kovacev. Can you tell me if she still lives upstairs?"

The woman shook her head. "Oh, no, no one lives there anymore."

Irene's shoulders fell. "Oh, okay."

"It's so sad what happened there. Some men came a few weeks ago and took away all his stuff."

Irene blinked at her. "Bobby Kovacev's stuff, you mean? But what about his wife?"

The lady frowned. "As far as I know, she died a long time ago."

"But—that's impossible. She never lived here?"

"No, he lived alone. Used to show me pictures of her. He carried around this terrible guilt, poor man. Said he came home from work one night back in Bosnia, and she'd been killed." She paused. "*By those people,*" she whispered. "*So terrible what happened over there.*"

Irene stared at her. The doctor had gotten it all wrong. The voices hadn't been telling Bobby to hurt his wife; they had been asking him why he didn't save her.

"Sorry I can't help you," the woman said.

"Did you find what you were looking for?" her father asked when she got in the car.

She thought about it. "I don't know."

"I have to tell you something," he said. "I gave some money to your friend before she left. To go visit her family." He chewed his lip and looked at her. "Are you upset? I know it's none of my business."

Irene opened her mouth to say something but changed her mind. There wasn't an escape for Bobby, and she couldn't go back to that dorm room and get out before the fire started, and her father couldn't bring her mother back. But there was still a chance for Yasmina to find her family again. She hoped Yasmina was already on a plane to Germany, with America and its corn and fast cars far below her.

"Oh, Dad, it's okay." She had this urge to get out of the car and switch places with him. She suddenly wanted nothing more than to give him the keys and let him drive her home, like he had when she was a little girl, when there was nothing she had to do except close her eyes and fall asleep.

Tonight Everything Will Be Quiet and Still

In three days, she'll be valedictorian of her high school class. She'll graduate in a white gown with a medal around her neck, on the football field behind the gym where her brother used to play. When the caps go up, her parents and the people in the stands will stand and cheer through hands cupped around their mouths. The band will lead them off the field and afterward the parking lot will be full of strangers she's known all her life.

One day, when she's older with a daughter of her own, she'll find the tape of her speech while she's cleaning out the garage. She'll put it in an old VCR player, and she'll consider her younger self the way you might recall a friend you used to know, someone you run into at a train station after many years have gone by. You chat for a while, but your train is leaving and you have to go, and you are sad because you know that you will never see her again.

◆ ◆ ◆

But that's not today. Today, she is spread out on the lawn behind her house in New Jersey, working on her speech. For now, the sun is shining, the sprinklers next door have erupted through the grass like geysers, and her mother is scrubbing pans in the kitchen. She calls something through the open window, and Lianne waves as if she's heard her.

This is the summer of last things. Her last grandfather is in the hospital. She expects she'll sleep with her boyfriend in August before she leaves for Cornell, and that things will change after that. She doesn't think she'll look at her house the same way again, or her room with its lavender wallpaper and dolphin light switch cover. So she tries to take it all in while she can—the flowers on the table; her mother's collection of Thomas Kinkade prints, the lights burning in the doorways; the way her father stoops to check the windows before bed, always in the same order. At night she reads a volume of British poetry her grandfather gave her. He bought the book in London during World War II, which was the defining event of his life. For all the years she can remember he has talked a lot about the war—and yet still said nothing meaningful about it at all. When he dies he'll be buried in Arlington, and he's asked that each family member put something in his coffin that reminds them of him, and the poetry book is the item she has chosen. She'd like to photocopy a few of the poems so she doesn't forget them, but she feels the purpose may be to give up something you cherish, like during Lent.

Her boyfriend's name is Joel. He graduated last year with her brother's class and is a freshman at the University of Maryland, currently studying abroad in Salamanca until July. She is not naïve enough to think he will stay faithful through three months in Spain, and Maryland is a long way from Ithaca; they've talked about splitting up in the fall. She doesn't love him and never will, but she'd still like to be with him once, just to know what it's like.

Given their mutual friends, they should be closer than they are. Lianne is dating someone her brother Jack used to know, and Jack is dating a girl from her class, a Jewish girl named Greta Rosen. Greta is a quiet, thoughtful student, someone who keeps her head down, studies hard, and goes to temple on Friday night. As far as Lianne knows, Greta doesn't have many close friends. Her father has a medical degree but works as an artist, drawing pictures for medical textbooks. Lianne suspects he pushes Greta hard because he couldn't make it as a doctor and thinks she will. Greta has taken more hard sciences than Lianne has, which is how she ended up second in the class and not first. Still, though, they've never really hung out just the two of them, even though they've been to each other's birthday parties every year since kindergarten.

It's unusual where they come from for a Jew to date a Catholic. The girls can be friends with each other, but Jewish girls never go out with Catholic guys, and Greta has to keep Jack a secret from her parents. They met over spring break and have only been dating since March, but he's already in love with her. He's come home from West Point for his summer leave to be with her.

◆ ◆ ◆

On this particular day of summer, three days before Lianne's graduation, Jack comes outside and stands over her on the lawn. He has his hands on his hips and his shadow makes the shape of wings. His stance reminds Lianne of the time when he was sixteen that she talked him out of jumping off the roof after a fight at school. He had broken the other boy's jaw, and the ambulance had come. Jack stood there in front of the pink late-afternoon sun, his hands at his waist like Peter Pan at the window of the nursery. Afterward he said he was high, he thought he could fly, but Lianne knew he'd never taken those kinds of drugs. That night he came into her room when their parents were asleep and curled up at the foot of her bed with his head on her ankle. He was wearing his Superman pajamas and looked like a nine-year-old boy.

Jack wants to know if Lianne can drive him to Greta's house and pick him up again later. Greta's parents are away for the weekend, he says, so they might be drinking. Greta lives on the other side of town, in what could be called the country, in that the nearest house is a half mile away and cell phones don't work there. Greta's house, though small, is on a lake and has a swimming dock just off the yard. At a birthday party when they were in fifth grade, Lianne and Greta were paired up in a swimming relay and won a trophy Greta's dad had made that said "Number One Team" on the plaque.

By the time Lianne drops Jack off, it's late afternoon and the water swells with light. "I'm not coming to get you if it's after midnight."

"I know," he says.

"I'm serious."

"I *know*."

Greta comes outside in a white sweater, hugging herself around the waist, even though it's very warm. Her dark hair is pulled back into a ponytail, and her knapsack is slung across her shoulder. "Hey, Lianne," she says. She reaches into her bag and takes out a heavy book. "Will you take my yearbook home tonight and sign it for me?"

Jack puts his hand on her back and holds it there as they cross the front lawn.

† † †

Later, Lianne's parents go out to a party. Lianne orders a pizza and waits on the porch for it to arrive. She likes being outside in this kind of quiet—that low-light, early-summer kind of quiet—when all along the street people are emerging for walks. They all pass by slowly and reverently, as if in worship of the season, as if they still can't believe it's possible that the year has brought them back here again. She wonders what Joel is doing on the other side of the world, and when the call will come about her grandfather—how sudden it will seem even though they've all been expecting it.

When the kitchen phone rings just before dark, she panics. Her parents aren't home yet, and if someone is calling to say come quickly, there's no time left, what will happen then? What if she's the only one to get there in time? She's not sure she can face him all alone like that, watch his body empty out.

But when she answers the phone, it's Jack's voice on the other end of the line. "Lianne," he says. "Come get me?" His voice is trembling.

"What happened? It's not even 8:30."

"Just come get me, okay?"

"I just called for a pizza—"

His voice breaks. "Greta broke up with me."

"What? Why?"

"I'll be waiting outside," he says and hangs up.

It's twenty-one minutes from Lianne's driveway to Greta's. Greta's house is set back about a quarter mile from the road, hidden by trees. By the time Lianne gets there the night is black as tar, and there are no streetlights in this part of town. As Lianne reaches the turn, she knows something is wrong. There's a flicker of light in the distance, like metal turned against the sun.

She sees the fire when her car breaks through the trees. It has consumed a quarter of the second floor already; flames are twisting behind the windows. She expects Jack and Greta to be waiting outside on the front lawn, but there's no sign of either of them. Lianne gets out of the car and stands in the driveway, calling their names, then goes around to the back of the house, where the fire hasn't reached yet, and tests the door. The knob is cool, but inside the kitchen is clogged with smoke. The noise of the fire upstairs is louder than she would have thought.

Still, she pushes her way inside and makes her way toward the phone. When she hears nothing on the other end of the line, she lets the receiver fall without hanging it up and runs through the smoke upstairs toward Greta's room, holding her sleeve against her mouth, afraid of what she might find there.

It's so hot she can taste the sweat dripping into the corner of her mouth. But by the time she reaches the top of the stairs, she's too late; the bedrooms are already consumed with fire. The flames are raw, hissing, volcanic. In books people describe them as red or orange but the fire Lianne sees is blue, the color of the deep end of the pool.

There's a window across from her, at the top of the stairs. Outside, she catches a glimpse of someone at the far edge of the backyard. She runs down the stairs and out the back door, choking in the hot summer air.

"Jack!" she cries, running across the lawn. "Is that you?"

Jack sits up, startled. He is filthy, covered in soot. "I didn't *do* this, Lianne!" he yells, as if she is accusing him of something. "She won't wake up!" he says. "I can't get her to wake up."

That's when Lianne sees Greta, unconscious and stretched out next to Jack in a long gray nightshirt and cotton panties that must once have been white. Her matching cotton bra is showing at the shoulder; it reminds Lianne of the training bras her mother used to buy her.

"The phone inside's not working," Lianne yells. "We need to call someone."

"No, no, it was working. I already called 911."

Lianne kneels down on the grass next to them. Neither of them knows CPR. That's when she notices the large purple bruise, the size of a peach, on Greta's upper arm. As if in a trance, she reaches out to touch it. Somehow all she can think is that Greta is supposed to sit next to her at graduation, and that the nearest hospital is the one where her grandfather is dying.

"Help me wake her up," she says. She starts pushing on Greta's chest.

"I've already tried that!" Jack yells. "You don't know how to do it any better than I do!"

They can hear the sirens through the trees.

"Go out to the road and meet them," Lianne says, and Jack grabs her arm, his eyes wide and scared.

"I was outside waiting for you. Then I saw the fire and I ran in and got her, but I couldn't wake her up. . ." There are tears on his cheeks. "I was *mad* at her for being in there. I don't know why I was mad at her. . ."

"Swear to me you didn't start the fire."

"Are you serious?"

He's never lied to her. "You stay," she says suddenly. "I'll go." Then she is running through the yard, toward the vehicles in the driveway, and behind her Jack has become so small, a figure she almost can't identify—just the outline of a boy, like someone cut out for a diorama.

◆ ◆ ◆

When the paramedics take her away in the ambulance, Greta is breathing, but barely. The entire second story of the house is a black shell; the driveway, thanks to so many police and fire trucks, is awash in light. Jack and Lianne are given wet cloths to wipe the soot off their faces. A police officer questions them while the fire fighters trudge through the smoking house.

"When I got here," Liane said, "they were on the lawn. The flames were up the curtains."

"She's covered in bruises," the officer says. "Do you know how that happened?"

Lianne shook her head. "I guess when Jack was carrying her out of the house."

The officer hands them two bottles of water. "It's a damn miracle you all got out," he says.

◆ ◆ ◆

On a Tuesday morning, Lianne will graduate in a white gown with a medal around her neck, on the football field behind the gym where Jack used to be halfback. Greta won't be there; she'll be given her diploma in the hospital, in a private ceremony. "After Jack left, she took a sleeping pill," Greta's parents will explain about the accident, "and forgot to blow out the candle by the window. It's a miracle she's alive."

Midway through Lianne's speech, the events of that night, and her own part in them, will impress themselves on her; she will start to cry and interrupt her address to say it is only right that she talk about Greta, that she is sorry she couldn't save her. People will come up to her afterward, offering her their hands, and tell her but she *did* save Greta—if it wasn't for Lianne and Jack, Greta would be dead. They'll never realize she was talking about something else entirely: that she had thought herself one kind of person and had proven herself another, that she never asked the questions she should have because she didn't actually want to know.

She won't sleep with Joel after all. She will be all right in college, although there will be moments when she'll want to call home in the middle of the night. In a year Jack will decide to leave West Point for a regular college, and after graduation he'll find a good job as a loan officer in New York, good enough to afford a two-bedroom apartment in Brooklyn. After a while, he'll meet a girl, and one day he'll marry her. They'll exchange rings in a church that smells like new paint and roses.

They won't see their grandfather alive again, which Lianne will be thankful for, because she knows the dying can see things other people can't. What she will see is Greta's face in coffee shops all over the city, and in the rearview mirror of her car as she pulls away from traffic lights. She will see her so often that when she does really run into her, in a place as ordinary as a D'Agostino supermarket in New York City, she almost keeps walking. She stops only when she sees the scar on her throat from the tube the paramedics inserted all those years ago, small and dark as a quarter.

"Lianne?" Greta reaches out with a hug. She is a little older, a little heavier. "What are you *doing* here?"

They talk about small things—college, the weather—and though Lianne knows she should ask about work, health, family, kids, she can barely mutter, "I'm so sorry, I'm late for an appointment." She knows she should be relieved by the encounter—Greta practically shining in the ordinariness of her life—but instead all Lianne can think of is the seventeen-year-old girl she used to be before the fire, how badly she wishes she could take Greta by the hands.

Greta pulls out a white business card and writes her home address on the back with a plastic pen. "I'm still in Jersey. Stop by sometime if you're ever in the neighborhood."

"Of course."

"I mean it."

"I know," Lianne says, but she won't come, and she won't see Greta again. But she does send Greta her old yearbook wrapped in white tissue paper, the one she never gave back, with a note on the autograph page that says, "I hope most of all you have someone who really loves you."

Eventually Jack and his wife will have two children, and Lianne, living twelve houses down on Flatbush Avenue, will have three of her own. And Jack's children and Lianne's will play together on summer nights, when it is so still and quiet she'll want to whisper that things could have been so different, she could have been a million miles away from here.

Waiting for the Creel

The women had taken a hotel up in Maine, where the lobsters were. The room had a double bed and a kitchenette, and they slept with their backs to each other, the cool night air coming in the open window from the bay.

When they got dressed, Sofia always turned toward the wall. She didn't like being seen or seeing Alice either, because Alice had a smaller waistline and pecan-brown hair and smooth skin under her eyes. When Sofia was young, she had been beautiful. But she was old now. And there was nothing she could do about that.

Outside the hotel, three boys shot marbles on the sidewalk. The pavement steamed in the heat. It was already July; the ocean glistened in pewter.

After they dressed, the women went to the café and ate breakfast. The café was two blocks from the beach, and the smell of bread drifted out to the street. Through the windows Sofia could see fresh scones cooling on the countertop; sweets were twisted in wax paper and sold in white boxes.

The women asked for slices of brown bread with butter and sat in a yellow booth. They ate in silence. Sofia spilled crumbs onto the lap of her skirt and brushed them off with a napkin. Alice called the waitress over. She ordered more tea and a croissant. "I do not understand that you are so skinny," Sofia said, squeezing her thigh. "Since I become sixty I get to be so fat. And then I keep getting fatter."

Past the window, young women toted babies and beach chairs and sandwiches in paper bags. They slid in and out of the light as they passed under the purple awnings of the shops.

Alice watched them make their way toward the beach. She wore silver hoop earrings, tarnished now because she pulled on them when her nerves got to her. "You know," she said after a moment, lifting a finger to her ear, "if my brother hadn't married you, I don't know where he'd be now." She poured a packet of sugar into her tea. "If that's any help at all. Maybe it's not."

When they had paid the bill, Alice said they should rent a surrey. "Do they make these surreys for two?" Sofia asked. "I thought always they were for four." Alice said she thought so, in New Jersey at least she'd seen them. She told Sofia how one summer, when Katie was eight, they rented one from the place next to Steel's Fudge. That was before the beach had been dredged, she said, and the water came all the way up underneath the boardwalk, and you could see it through the cracks in the boards. She said Katie had noticed something, and they went to the edge to look in, and there was a little glass bottle floating in the water with a note in it.

Alice said, "Katie crawled under the rail and fished the bottle out of the water, and it turns out it had come all the way from Ireland and had been floating in the sea for thirty-something years. The Guinness Brewery had thrown a whole bunch of bottles into the ocean, I guess, in 1959, to mark their bicentennial. That was what the note said. But anyway, Katie still has it, I'm sure."

Katie was in Afghanistan now, working in army intelligence. Her husband was also in the army, but they deployed on alternating schedules, so they rarely saw each other. Sofia wondered whether that kind of a marriage could last.

The man who rented the surreys was huddled over the desk, cracking pistachio shells into a takeout carton. Alice tapped the window, and he came outside. He was heavyset, his face raw and chafed from the sun.

"Do you have surreys for two people?" Alice asked him, and he laughed and said, yes, that was mostly what he had.

They paid $15 for an hour. They pedaled down the boardwalk past the shops, which were boarded up until noon, and past the joggers in their white-laced trainers. Beside them, on the beach, women led dogs on retractable leashes.

When Sofia's phone rang in her purse, they pulled over to the side. Sofia got out of the surrey and went over to the railing, where Alice couldn't hear. She watched the gulls patrolling the beaches for food, stirring the sand with their feet. They walked with soldiers' steps.

After a minute Sofia closed the phone and climbed back into her seat. She told Alice, "It was Robert." He wanted to know if she had gotten his suit from the dry cleaners, and if she did where had she put it.

"Do you wish you were there with him?" Alice asked.

"No," Sofia said. "No. I do not want to be there." She brought her fingers to the wrinkles on her forehead.

"Well, that's what you said before. I just wanted to be sure. I had my doubts about coming up here while all that was going on."

"But this is *why* we have come. Because all that is going on."

"No, you're right," Alice said, nodding. "I just feel bad for him. She was just a child. And there was nothing he could do."

"Yes. He a good man and I wish it had not been him there that night who found her. But it was. And I do not need to be there now to see the fingers pointed to him."

Alice thought about this. She pedaled and watched the waves roll over in the ocean. "It would have been right to go to the funeral, though," she said at last.

They stopped again to use the toilet and Sofia ran the sink while she modeled her hips in front of the mirror. "These are no good," she said when Alice came to wash her hands.

◆ ◆ ◆

When Sofia came from Hungary, she was twenty-three. She traveled by boat with her mother. They left from a port in Gdansk, Poland and came to New Jersey. They rented a room at the top of a restaurant and took English classes. But the crossing had been rough, and her mother became sick and mostly stayed at home. Sofia found a receptionist's job at a Ford dealership in Ocean City. She was not a typist yet. In Hungary, other women had told her typing could be taught but a pretty face could not. In America she found they were right.

She liked the smell of the beach and the salt because these things were new to her. She did not mind always cleaning the film from the windshields of the cars in the lot. From her desk she could watch the Ferris wheel turn above the city, and when the moon came out the lamps were lit on the boardwalk. Still, she didn't like leaving her mother alone in the apartment every day.

At night, they were always afraid. This was the late 1950s, and it was rare for two women to live alone without any men. They bought a television for the noise it made, which distracted them from their fears, and they pushed their two small beds together to form one. Her mother asked her constantly about marriage, pressing her: "You *must* marry, Sofia. When are you going to marry?" When she could not sleep her mother paced the kitchen and cried into her hands. "We will be sent back, I know it, tomorrow they will come," she said.

Sofia said don't worry, did she not see she was a beautiful girl? She thought of Robert, the security guard at work, who stuttered when he spoke to her and cleaned her desk when she went home for the night. She had no difficulty attracting men. Still, she would not marry just anyone. She told her mother she would take all the time she pleased.

Some weeks later a young businessman came into the showroom. He carried a leather briefcase and held his sunglasses between his fingers. His dark hair was combed back, and he smiled at her but went to sit down in the lounge instead of examining the cars. He spent a quarter of an hour looking at brochures and drinking coffee and watching Sofia as she typed. He was handsome. He had that bronzed American skin and his trouser legs were well ironed and creased at the shin.

She came over to pour him more coffee. "Do you look to buy car?" she asked him. He raised his eyebrows hearing her accent and smiled again.

This is a beautiful man, she thought. Maybe I will go to dinner with him. We will see.

But he did not ask her to dinner. Instead he talked about his job. He said he worked for a company that made mannequins.

"Mannequin?" she said. She did not know this word yet.

"Yes. You know. Dolls, for store windows. Do you understand?"

"Oh. Yes, yes," she said, although she wasn't quite sure.

He said he wanted to make a mannequin out of her. Could he take her measurements and would she come in tomorrow to do the photographs? He would pay her $200.

That was more than she made in three weeks of work. "Oh," she said, flustered. "But how I do this? Must I be . . . undressed?"

"Well, yes," he said. "But not completely. You wear, you know—your undergarments."

She did not tell her mother. She called in sick to work and met him at a photographer's studio in Trenton the next day. The room was full of men, and she was ashamed. She had never let a man see her undressed. An assistant, the only woman in the studio, gave her a robe to wear, but underneath she felt exposed.

She sat on a stage with her arms draped over her knees while the men took her photograph and shaped the wire for the body. No one tried to touch her. They told her not to be nervous, she was beautiful; they were all very professional. Next they told her to hold out her hands. They soaked them in water and plaster and a mold was cast. By the time this was done she was shivering. They told her not the worry, the rest of her body would be cast in clay from the photographs. She could go home now.

Rafael, the man who had come to the dealership, met her at the door to her dressing room to give her the check. He said did she know she could be a model? She was tall and had the right form. He told her where to look for casting calls.

She thought, after that, he might come back to see her again. He might call. But two weeks passed, and still she had not heard from him. She decided to go to a casting at Harrah's in Atlantic City, because men like him went to Atlantic City a lot, and she hoped he might be there.

She did not see him there. But she was hired for a job in a catalogue, modeling jewelry.

Over the next few months she made enough money from these catalogue jobs to lease a car for her mother so she could leave the apartment while Sofia was at work. But her mother refused to accept the car. She called her daughter a whore and said she didn't raise her to show her body like a street girl.

It wasn't long before Sofia began auditioning as an actress. She was cast as a cocktail waitress in a movie being filmed in one of the casinos. She had no lines herself, but a well-known actor would touch her arm as she passed and say, "Hey, could I get a beer?"

Robert agreed to rehearse with her. She took a tray from the employee kitchen in the dealership and practiced walking while she balanced four glasses. She laughed when Robert tried to play the lead. He was nothing like the actor. But he watched her carefully as she practiced, and was very thoughtful with his critiques.

The evening before her first day of shooting she received a call from the casting director. He was sorry, he said, but he couldn't use her in the film. "I know you are not here legally, Sofia. Really, please be careful. There are ways of finding these things out."

She wanted to tell him she was in the JC Penney's catalogue, of course she was an American. She was in the JC Penney's catalogue! But she couldn't find the words.

For months after she was fired from the film, she was terrified. She refused to answer the phone, to go to the door. She stayed up at night watching the window for approaching headlights.

In April, her mother died in her sleep.

It was too much to bear. She panicked that she would be sent back to Hungary alone; her brother had died the month before, and she had no family there anymore.

She thought of Rafael, who didn't want her, who had never come back. Then she remembered Robert. There was always Robert.

◆ ◆ ◆

After returning the surrey, the women loaded three lobster traps into the car and drove out to the launch site by the bay. They paid for a three-day rental on a motorboat. They drove to the edge of the bay, where the ocean began. Alice explained to Sofia that the trap was called a creel. It had a wooden frame surrounded by rope mesh, and a small fish placed inside the frame was supposed to attract the lobsters.

It had been Alice's idea to go to lobster hunting. When she was a child, her and Robert's grandparents lived in a house near this bay, and their father had taught them how to lay the cages.

"How long must we wait for to check them again?" Sofia asked when they had lowered all the traps. The buoys bobbed like dolls' heads by the side of the boat.

"It'll take about two days probably," Alice said. She rinsed her hands in the water. "We'll come back on Saturday, and if we've caught anything, we'll cook it up for dinner Saturday night."

When the sun was hot overhead, they unwrapped their sandwiches and ate them with warm soda and chips. They lay with their sun hats over their eyes and rested for a while, listening to the water lapping against the rudder. Greenflies milled over the marshland behind them.

"You're going to leave him, aren't you," Alice said. It wasn't a question.

Sofia sat up. She was angered by Alice's frankness. "Why would I do this, Alice? You tell me."

"You don't love him anymore. You blame him for what happened. I'm not accusing you. I'd blame him too. It was his *job*. He should have been there to stop it."

Sofia shook her head. She leaned forward and took Alice's arm. "This is problem for me, Alice. I love him too much to go. All these years I have looked for the reason to go and now when I have such a reason, I cannot leave."

"Oh," Alice said. "I never knew you felt like that."

"He is fired now. He has no job."

"I know. I'll give you some money if you need it."

"No, no." She waved her hand. "I have saved some away. When my brother died in Hungary, he was almost rich man."

"I didn't know," Alice said. "I don't think Robert ever mentioned it."

The sun blared over their heads, bleaching the sand. Alice wiped her forehead with the back of her hand. Suddenly she leaned forward. "The night it happened. I know he was with another woman. He was, wasn't he, Sofia?"

Sofia shrugged. "Let us go now, Alice, yes?"

"Yes," Alice said, putting her hand on Sofia's arm. "All right."

◆ ◆ ◆

For six years Robert had been working the night shift as the security guard at the Wonderland Pier on the Ocean City boardwalk. He signed in at 9, when the rides were closing down, and stayed until 7 the next morning. He often talked to Sofia, privately, about how much he disliked it. It was the horses, he said. The carousel. The way they looked in the dark. "They're creepy," he said.

"Maybe you quit?" Sofia suggested. "Go work somewhere else."

"No," he said. "If I stay ten years I'll get retirement. I can stick it out till then."

In his six years on the job nothing more serious had happened than some teenagers breaking in once to walk the maze in the mirror house. But then one of the engineers found the body of a nine-year-old girl in the center of the carousel, where the motors ran. She lay naked, twisted between the gears. She had been killed, the police determined, in the fairground several nights earlier. It had happened not far from the carousel; the spot was marked with her blood. The carousel had been running for three days with her body trapped inside.

The park was closed down. Yellow tape surrounded the crime scene. Robert was held by the Ocean City police and interrogated for seven hours. Where were you when this happened? Did you not hear her yell? Nothing?

Robert kept his head in his hands. "I don't know," he said. "I just don't know."

They had no evidence to hold him. His DNA was not on the body. He was released when the lab confirmed that the girl's bruises had been made by someone swinging from the right. Robert was left-handed.

But still, he had been marked. A child had died under his watch.

✦ ✦ ✦

The women drove around the town looking at the old houses. "I came to a baptism here once," Alice said, pointing to a squat brick church. "I was just a child. The party was in the yard afterward. It was a beautiful party."

Some of the houses were for sale. Red balloons had been tied to the mailbox of a Victorian farmhouse. Alice stopped the car. "It's an open house—see the sign? Let's go inside."

"Well—" Sofia began, but followed her anyway across the lawn.

They were greeted at the door by a plump brunette in a yellow blazer and skirt. She stood for a moment in a pose of shyness and pride, and then, remembering herself, hurried backward to let them pass. "Oh, please, come inside." She craned her neck to scan the street behind them. She said, embarrassed then, "You're my first of the day, actually."

In the kitchen a plate had been set out with salami and cheese, and wine in plastic cups. Red paper napkins were spread on the table like playing cards. The women passed slowly through the rooms, the snacks cupped inside napkins in their palms. The agent explained that the house was owned by an elderly couple, married for fifty years, who wanted to retire down south.

"Oh?" Alice mused. "Can it come furnished?" She trailed her finger along the arm of a dining chair. Its curve was the shape of a swan's back.

Oh, yes, she said, absolutely it could. She pointed out a vanity set made of white oak. It had been shipped from Berlin, she told Alice, just before the Second World War.

In the dining room the chandelier drooped within an arm's reach, and the doorway was narrow, but the windows had been cut wide and the sun buttered the tabletop and the bureau. Sofia determined the curtains had been often left open; the paintings on the walls had ripened almost to white.

While they were wandering upstairs, Sofia's phone rang. She excused herself and went outside to take the call, telling Alice she would meet her by the car.

It was Robert again. He said the funeral had gone all right. At least no one had said anything to him. And Alice's husband, Gene, had come by the house afterward. "Will you be home soon?" he asked at last.

"Sunday probably. We must catch the lobsters first."

"Oh, all right." There was silence. "Are you having a good time then?"

"A lovely time."

"What are you doing now?" he asked.

"We are out to take a walk," she said.

"Well, I won't keep you. But I'll see you soon?"

"Yes," she said. "See you soon." She told him goodbye and waited by the curb for Alice. In a few minutes the front door opened and Alice emerged, her arms full of colorful brochures. The agent stood at the door, waving, until they had gotten into the car.

Sofia climbed into the passenger seat. "It was charming, yes?"

Alice tightened the strap on her seatbelt. "We really should buy it, don't you think?" She turned toward Sofia. Her eyes glistened. "Really, we should."

Sofia was stricken. "Oh, I do not know about this. What about Robert? What about Katie and Gene?"

"Well, we could do a timeshare. Or we could come in the fall for a while, to see the colors change, and then rent it out for the summers."

"Perhaps," Sofia mused, and left it at that. If she said nothing more, she thought, Alice would forget the proposal in a day or two. She turned to the window. She counted the mailboxes they passed.

But then, as they were driving, she remembered the way Robert mixed the paper and the aluminum together in the recycling bin when he wasn't supposed to, and how he always threw dirty shirts back into drawers, and all the times the neighbors had asked her over the years, "Sofia, when *will* there be a baby?" until she had grown too old and was more ashamed that they'd stopped asking than she'd been when they had. And as they drove past the rows of houses, their garden walls choked with ivy, surrounded by gray rocks that dipped into the sea, she said, "Okay, Alice, let us do it," and Alice said really, was she certain? and Sofia said yes, she had the money and she was sure.

They ate their dinner on the beach, picking calamari and french fries from paper bags. They talked about their plans for the house. Alice made sketches on the back of a takeout carton. "Of course, we'll have to renovate the kitchen," she said, "and have the furniture appraised so we can know what to keep. But the outside has already been repainted, and that's a start."

Sofia lay down with her cheek against the sand and thought of the fall in Maine, the trees scalded with color.

◆ ◆ ◆

That night, there was a storm over the ocean. Sofia awoke to the rush of water on the sidewalk. She got out of bed and opened the window. Outside, she could see two birds huddled in the tree, their wings drooping with rain.

She knelt by Alice's side of the bed and touched her shoulder. "Alice," she said. "Alice."

Alice murmured, turning onto her stomach.

"Alice, let us go out to check the traps now, yes?"

"It's too early," Alice said into the pillow. She groped around the table for the clock: 3 a.m. "Wait until the morning."

"It is morning."

"You're crazy, Sofia. Go back to sleep."

Sofia sat in the armchair, her knees pulled to her chest, smoking a cigarette. After an hour Alice opened her eyes again and saw Sofia's dark shape folded up in the chair. She kicked the covers from her knees. "Jesus, Sofia. You scared me. What are you doing there?"

"I cannot sleep," she said.

"Why not?"

She shrugged. "I just keep thinking about those traps, I guess."

Alice got out of bed and lifted the curtain from the window. She leaned her elbow on the sill and stretched her hand outside, palm up. "The rain's stopped," she said. She turned on the lamp and looked at Sofia. "Are you in a hurry to get back home? Is that it?"

Sofia shrugged again.

Alice sighed and took the boat key from the ashtray by the bed. "Fine. Let's go now."

They dressed in silence and then got into the car and drove out to the launch site. It was the middle of the night, but the moon and the streetlamps cast a hazy white light on the water. Their boat was tied by the dock. It rocked back and forth as the bay swelled underneath. The dark backs of the fish moved under the surface of the water.

Sofia turned on the flashlight. Alice ran the ignition, and they both jumped at the sound, which seemed louder than it should in the stillness of the night. Across the bay, a swarm of kingfishers spiraled into the air, flapping wildly.

"I have a feeling," Sofia said, grinning, "that we have caught many lobsters." She gripped the windshield as Alice maneuvered the boat away from the dock. "This will be first lobster I eat, ever."

"Ever?"

"And we will catch the lobsters, and buy the house, and come here many times again, yes?"

Alice said, "You better wait to tell Robert. He's going to lose it when you tell him how much money it will cost."

They followed the shoreline for a while, but as they neared the edge of the bay there were fewer and fewer houses, and fewer streetlamps, and eventually Sofia's flashlight was the only guide they had.

Suddenly Alice made a sharp left. The spray caught the back of Sofia's neck.

"Where are you going?" Sofia asked. "I pointed over there, no?" She wiggled the flashlight, gesturing to the right.

"But you didn't," Alice insisted. "You pointed left."

She slowed the boat to a stop. In the water ahead of them, two small circles of light bobbed on the black surface. The circles were the size of onions. As the wake from the boat crossed over them, they moved like jellyfish, wrinkling and stretching.

Sofia leaned over to look and then drew back. "What is that?"

Alice looked desperately around them for the source of the light. They were only about twenty feet from the shore, but there was no movement along either side. She turned back to the water. "I think it's coming from *underneath*," she said finally.

Sofia laughed. "Like—a ghost?"

The boat swayed. Alice gripped the steering wheel, lowering herself into the seat. "No, Sofia. I think those are *headlights*."

Sofia grabbed Alice's elbow.

"Look," Alice said. "I'm sure of it." She was shaking now. "There's something down there."

"What should we do?" Sofia pressed. "Can we do anything?"

Alice fumbled for her phone, but they were too close to the ocean now for any signal to come through.

"Oh, God, oh, *God*, Alice." Sofia rocked her head in her hands.

"I'm going to go in," Alice said. She pulled her arms out of the sleeves of her jacket. "What if there's someone down there?"

"It's too deep. You won't make it."

"I *have* to," Alice huffed. She was halfway undressed now. Her eyes moved about wildly. "People could be stuck inside."

Sofia held her wrist. "Don't. Don't leave me here."

"I have to. I think I hear something." Alice pulled free and jumped into the water, disappearing into the blackness. As her body crossed the beams underneath the water the lights disappeared and reappeared, flickering on and off like signal lanterns. Sofia curled into a ball on the floor of the boat.

When Alice reappeared, she was gasping for breath. "I can't get down there," she yelled. "It's too deep. We'll have to go to shore and call the police." She swam around to the back of the boat, lowered the ladder, and climbed inside.

As they sped back toward the dock, Sofia's phone picked up a signal. She called 911, her voice frantic. "You must come," she said. "There is a car in the water." Alice tried to pull the boat up against the dock, but she ran the bow into the rail. She had to run the boat aground on the beach next to the lot so they could climb out.

Then they had nothing to do but wait. Alice was shivering. They got into the car and Sofia turned the heat on high.

"Jesus, how long does it take?" Alice said. She got out of the car and began pacing the dock. When they heard the sirens, Sofia got out of the car also and stood huddled against the hood, her jacket wrapped around her shoulders. A Coast Guard boat arrived at the same time as the police car.

Alice and Sofia climbed into one of the Coast Guard boats, and Alice pointed out the path they had taken along the shore. "It's just up this way. We were looking for our lobster traps . . ." She turned to man beside her, as if seeking his forgiveness.

They drove for what seemed like an hour. The water was brighter now, illuminated by the powerful lamps of the bigger boats that had joined them. Then Sofia waved her hand. "Wait, stop. It is here."

They slowed the boat. The lights appeared, nodding under the surface of the water. The water lay now like a dead thing.

The men exchanged glances. One of them unclipped the radio from his belt and called the control station on shore. Then he called the driver of the other boat. The second man zipped his wetsuit to the chin and began checking the air in the diving tanks. Then he looked up, frowning. "You're going to have to wait on shore," he told the women. "We'll have the other boat take you back now."

"No!" Alice protested, taking his arm. "Please. We have to see if there's someone down there."

"Look, this isn't a show."

Alice was furious. "You just can't *do* that!" she cried. "We deserve to know!"

"Shhh," Sofia said, wrapping her arm around Alice's shoulders. "Come on." She led Alice onto the plank that connected the two boats. One of the Coast Guard officers reached out to help them across. He had soft hands. Alice pulled away.

They were offered a thermos of coffee. Alice took the thermos but left it unopened. She sat in stony silence, watching the reflection of the stars moving across its silver lid. The wind whirled around them. Sofia breathed into her cupped hands.

When they arrived at the dock they were met by a circus of colored lights. The parking lot was full of noise and people—two fire trucks had arrived, and more police cars, and a television news van. The reporter, checking the cameras, didn't notice the women as they stepped onto the dock. One of the police officers ushered them to the edge of the lot and asked them to wait in the picnic area across the road. He put his hand on Alice's wrist as he pointed.

"Don't touch me," she said.

The women went over and sat on top of a wooden table with their feet resting on the bench. Alice rubbed her arms fiercely, trying to stay warm.

Sofia reached over and took her hand. "I wonder if we will be interviewed for the television," she said at last.

"Who knows?"

"I do not know if I tell Robert about this. Probably I will not."

"Don't. He has a lot to think about right now."

More trucks had arrived. There were faces in the windows of the houses nearby. Probably, all along the shoreline of the bay, kitchen lights were turning on like dominoes, leading up to the spot they had just left.

Sofia sat with her hands clasped tightly in her lap. "Do you think he did it?"

"Do I think who did what?"

"Robert. Do you think he killed that girl?"

Alice was quiet. She watched the men and women running to and fro in the distance, their jackets blued by the siren lights. She pulled the sleeves of her own jacket over her hands. "I don't know." There was a silence and then Alice asked, "Are you going to leave him?"

Sofia said nothing.

"Are you?" Alice pressed.

"No," Sofia said finally.

After a moment Alice stood up. "This is ridiculous. I'm going over there to find out what's happening."

One of the fire fighters was standing on the far edge of the dock, smoking a cigarette. Alice came up behind him and stood with her hands on her hips. "What are you doing?" she demanded furiously. "How can you just be standing here?"

The man turned and stepped backward, surprised. When he saw Alice, he tapped the cigarette over his palm and dumped the ashes into the bay. "Who are you?" he asked.

"You're just standing here. What about the car? You're just—" Alice began to cry.

The man reached out and touched her shoulder, lightly. She came closer and put her head against his chest. She was sobbing now. He patted her head. Then he put his arm around her. "Look, it's all right, lady," he said. "It was just a car."

Alice looked up at him. "What do you mean?"

"There wasn't anyone inside. The car was empty. Didn't you know?"

She pulled away. "But how is that *possible*? How does an empty car get to the middle of the bay?"

"It could have been stolen," he said, and shrugged. "The driver could have run it in there on purpose. Or he could have gone in with it and swum out the window, and either way he's long gone now. Things like that happen."

"Oh," Alice whispered. "Oh."

"Oh, thank God," Sofia breathed when Alice reported the news. "Alice. Alice? Let us go back now, yes? I think it is time to go."

◆ ◆ ◆

The women were quiet as they drove back to the hotel. When they pulled into the lot the sun was just starting to come out. The colors shimmered over the ocean.

Alice turned off the engine but didn't open her door. She sat with her hands on the steering wheel, staring down the street toward the boardwalk. "I really thought there would be someone in there," she said.

"Yes. I know."

"I thought we'd *saved* someone."

"Yes," Sofia said. "It is shame."

"It was just a stupid car."

They didn't stop for breakfast. Neither of them mentioned the lobsters, or the farmhouse they knew without discussing it they weren't going to buy anymore. They drove in the middle lane down the turnpike toward New Jersey, and on either side there were children peering out the back of minivans, and women in red sedans with bicycles tied to the roofs and dogs hanging their heads out the windows, bracing their tongues against the wind.

The Chimney

In the middle of the Ithaca hills, the towns are cut deep. People can get lost here. They stop for gas on the way to the city and forget to leave, and then one day they find they have spent their whole lives nestled in a valley at the base of the Adirondacks.

Every other evening Dominic runs under the bridge where the river meets the cemetery. Next to the jogging path, the hill slopes into the river and the water is smooth and gray as a metal spoon.

The path takes him inside the graveyard and around the perimeter. Every time he runs, Evie tells him it isn't respectful to run past people's graves. But today, for the first time since he began his weekly runs, there is a service going on, and he isn't sure whether the proper thing would be to slow down or keep running. From a distance he can't tell who is inside the casket, a man or a woman or even a child. At the front gate a woman is handing out rosaries and prayer cards.

Seeing the funeral reminds Dom of the woman who was kidnapped, two weeks ago, from the building next to his and Evie's. A man was going door-to-door selling phone cards, and she let him inside. But he didn't know that this woman's daughter, who was supposed to be asleep, was watching from the bedroom the whole time. Later the girl told the police the man stayed twenty minutes talking about the cards, showing her mother the catalogues and being very polite, and at the end of it all he said good night and then he took hold of her hair and pulled her out the door.

Since then, every time Dom leaves he checks to make sure Evie has locked the door after him.

There are eight people in the funeral party, seven women and a man, who is a wearing a white carnation through his buttonhole, his pants tucked into the backs of his shoes. He is bent over with his face in his hands, and the late sun casts a deep glow on the bald spot on the top of his head.

One by one the people step forward to throw roses into the grave. The man watches from the back of the group, taking the hand of a woman who is probably his wife, their skin cracked from age and sun. He is the last to step toward the grave to throw his rose.

Suddenly, he loses his balance and topples forward, almost into the grave. He lands on his knees at the edge of the hole; his glasses and the rose fall into the dirt where the casket has been lowered.

His wife rushes forward to help him stand. At first he can't get up, and he slips again in the damp soil. She takes him gently, lovingly, by the elbow. But when she turns, Dom can see quite clearly that it is not worry but pity on her face.

He wonders if she married him because she thought he was a good man, or because she knew he loved her, or because she got pregnant. When he is standing up again, she brushes the soil off her palms and slides her wrist through the loop of her purse.

◆ ◆ ◆

At home, Evie is sitting cross-legged on the sofa, her long hair wrapped around her arm like a sling. She has a square of canvas on her lap and she is tracing lines on the paper with the tips of her fingers, the way she sometimes touches Dom's face at night before they go to sleep.

She turns when Dom comes into the apartment. "Hi," she says. "How was the run?"

"It was fine." He leans over her shoulder and peers at the paper on her lap. "Is that the painting from the bedroom?"

"Yes," she says.

"Why did you pull it out of the frame?"

At the Rag Shop in Ithaca it costs $50 to mat and frame a picture that size. He bought the painting for Evie two years ago when she first moved to Ithaca to be with him. At the time, they had been together for only four months, but he got accepted at Ithaca College to do his PhD in art history, studying Russian Catholic icons. When he was younger he had seen an icon of Mary in an abbey in Pennsylvania that one of the brothers said had curative powers. Dom had been suffering from heart palpitations for as long as he could remember, but after he touched the cheek of the painting with his forefinger, from then on he never had a palpitation again. It could have just been a coincidence—but it also could have been something more.

Evie showed up at his door in Ithaca with all her things three weeks after he moved. It had been hard for her to leave her parents in Missouri, he knew, especially because her father was in the early stages of Alzheimer's. He should have given her a ring that day, but for some reason he didn't, and then the days got away from him, and the months, and it never happened.

Instead, the night she arrived, they went to a campus auction for charity and Evie fell in love with the painting. She said it reminded her of home. Dom won it for $500. In it, a hammock, tied from the lowest branch of a tree, hangs over an expanse of grass. Behind the tree, there is a house and a young woman sitting on the porch swing. It looks nothing like Evie's house and, to be honest, nothing much like Missouri, and she didn't seem to be able to explain what it was that drew her to it.

Later, that April, they went to Missouri to see her parents. It was a hot spring day, but after winters in Ithaca that kind of heat felt good. One afternoon while they were visiting, her father's mower broke down in the middle of the lawn. He leaned against the handle like a farmer pushing a plow, trying to get it to move. But it wouldn't budge. He stood there in a lunge, the sweat pouring down his face, his legs straddling the divide between the mowed and unmowed grass.

When Dom went outside, he saw her father's hands were shaking terribly. The doctors said his tremors were from Agent Orange exposure in Vietnam, and would only get worse. "Need any help?" Dom asked him, as casually as he could. Evie's father wiped his forehead with his handkerchief. "No," he said. "I'm fine."

It seems to Dom, standing over Evie's shoulder as she studies the painting, that something in it has upset her. He isn't sure whether it has to do with her father. It's confusing, certainly; she's been looking at it every day for two years.

"Dom," she says. "Someone came by while you were gone."

He freezes. "What do you mean?"

She looks at her lap and puts her fingers together in a chapel shape. "A man came to the door while you were out."

"Did you let him in?"

"Well, yes."

Dom's eyes widen. "Are you crazy?"

Evie sighs. "He wasn't the kidnapper. He was wearing a uniform."

"What do you mean, a uniform?"

"A military uniform."

"Army? Marines?"

She thinks about it. "I don't know."

He runs his hand through his hair. "You don't know," he repeats slowly. "Was it blue? Green?"

She chews the bottom of her lip. "I can't remember. It could have been brown."

"Jesus."

"He asked if he could see the painting. He said he had painted it, and he had gotten our address from the school auction, and it would mean a lot to him if he could just see it for a minute."

Dom paces to the other side of the room and back again. "I can't believe you are not fucking dead. There's a crazy person out there snatching women just like you."

Evie frowns. "He wasn't dangerous. He was *crying*."

"Why the hell was he crying?"

"I don't know. But I took him into the bedroom and he just stood there in the corner looking at the painting. Then he sat down on the floor for a minute and closed his eyes. Then he stood up again, said thank you, and left."

"That's it? He left? And he didn't say anything else?"

"Well, no."

"But you must have talked about something. About the painting, at least. Who the woman is."

Evie shook her head. "He just—looked at it. Like it was everything to him. I offered to give it to him, but he wouldn't take it."

"Evie, that's *our* fucking painting. It cost $500."

She comes toward him and takes his face in her hands. "But don't you think it's beautiful? For something you create to have that kind of power over you? You and me have each other, Dom. But I got the feeling he didn't have anyone, except maybe that woman in the painting."

"If it meant so much to him, why did he sell it?"

Evie lies down on the sofa and puts her hand over her eyes. "I *want* that, Dom," she says.

"I should call the police. He could have been the kidnapper." He picks up the phone.

"You can't report a man who knocks at your door and is invited to come in." She gets up and takes the phone out of his hand.

When she touches his hand, he feels something come over him. He takes hold of her wrist and pushes her against the refrigerator. His heart is racing, breaking. "Don't lie to me." His voice cracks. "Did you do anything with him?"

Evie doesn't flinch. "You're crazy. You're ridiculous."

"Did anything happen?"

She looks straight at him, hard into his eyes, and says, "No."

Dom's shoulders fall and he lets her go. She runs into the bathroom and turns the sink on. "Evie, let me in!" he pleads with her, jiggling the handle. "Damnit, Evie, open the door!" Finally he sits down and waits for her in the hallway, on the tiles with his back against the wall. The dirt from his running shoes—from the cemetery—is all over the hallway floor.

"I want to go home." Her voice is muffled through the door.

Dom leans against it. "Don't go. Stay with me. Don't go."

◆ ◆ ◆

When he wakes up, he is still on the hallway floor. Evie is asleep in the bedroom. The bedroom floor is covered with the little canvas pieces of their painting. He gets on his knees and tries to fit the bits back together, thinking of her fingers, as thin as dandelion stems, as she sliced the scissors into the hammock and the house and the tiny beautiful woman.

Nights are always hard to get through. He's tried pills and hypnosis and nothing works. In bed, as Evie is drifting off to sleep, sometimes he whispers to her, "Don't go yet, please." He knows he sounds weak and desperate. It frightens him, being left behind. He wants to get to where she is, but he can't.

Where is she, exactly? She's in a place somewhere between waking and sleeping, that blue twilit chimney where you can still hear voices from the place you left but they are very far away. And it's like she can keep going, into wherever she goes when she sleeps, or she can go back to him and take him with her. She just has to choose.

The Wedding

I met Liam in Pennsylvania. We were on inner tubes, spinning down the Delaware River, but I was far ahead and moving faster with the current because I was lighter. I noticed him because he had only one leg. He was young, and it was the '70s, so you knew it was the war. He was getting farther behind me, and when I went around a bend he disappeared from view.

I was twenty-two and just out of nursing school. My friend Meg and I had taken jobs in a hospital down in Charlotte, but before we left, we spent a weekend camping on the banks of the river.

Later, he and I saw each other again at the campsite. Liam was staying in the tent next to ours. He was vacationing with his niece, and we started talking by the fire while Meg braided the little girl's hair. He had a prosthetic leg, and he attached it before coming out to the fire.

He'd lost his leg in Khe Sanh in 1968, he said. He had only been there nine days when it happened, and then he was hot hoisted out and spent three weeks in the woods in France before going home, in a chateau they were using as a hospital.

"Fuckin' Vietnam," he said. "They took my leg and everything else."

"Does it hurt?" I asked him, rolling a hot dog over the flames. The war had just ended, and it was all anyone seemed to talk about.

He said, "Damn right. After all these years, too."

Later, in the middle of the night, he called out in his sleep. I crawled through the flap into his tent. He was cursing and rolling with the pain. The little girl was upright, her hands clasped in her lap, terrified.

"Shh," I told him, putting my fingers on his hip. "It's all right."

I stayed with him for an hour, rubbing the stump where his limb would have been. I gave him a pill for the pain. When he shook his

head, I told him, "Take it. I'm a nurse," as if that made any difference, when pills like that were as easy to buy in those days as candy.

I saw between his lashes the beginning of tears. "I didn't actually do
anything," he said. "I wasn't a hero, if that's what you're thinking."

"Okay," I said. "Well, it doesn't matter now."

"Do you think it will hurt like this forever?"

The pill knocked him out before I could figure out what to tell him.

◆ ◆ ◆

The next morning, I decided not to move to Charlotte. Meg left
without me. It would be almost a year before she would speak to me
again. Liam was teaching in a high school in Franklin, New Jersey,
and I took a job in a hospital in the town next to his. I moved back
into my mother's house in Pequannock. Everything was just as I'd
left it—the brown and yellow carpet, my poster of Rock Hudson
still on the bedroom wall.

In the evenings my mother and I ate spaghetti on tray tables by the
television. I slept with my hair in curlers and stared at the bathroom
light coming in underneath the door.

Liam never stayed the night, except for one time. We'd come home
from the movies drunk and laughing, grabbing onto each other.

"That's it," my mother told him. "You can't drive home like this."
She brought the cot up from the basement and Liam slept in the
living room by the fireplace.

"Thank you, ma'am, thank you," Liam said, his eyes shiny with
the liquor. We fell onto the floor, laughing.

◆ ◆ ◆

We were together for three years. We never lived together; for three
years we just dated like teenagers. In the middle of the night we
snuck into my room sometimes while my mother slept in the room
next door. We went to the movies; in the summers we went to the
New Jersey State Fair, where old men sent ducks around a pool with
prizes attached to their bottoms. We ate ice from paper cones and
bought painted flowerpots we weren't really going to use.

◆ ◆ ◆

In the evening once, in the park, he chased a firefly over the pond. I remember he ran all the way into the water to catch it. There he was, standing up to his waist in water with the algae around his belt, and he blew on this fist and rolled the fly from his hand like dice— *one, two, three.* I laughed. "Why do you do that? That poor thing."

He kissed the tips of his fingers. "It's good luck," he said, and shrugged. "Most of life is about luck."

◆ ◆ ◆

Liam taught home economics at Franklin High School. He did it because in the army he had been a cook. That was what they sent him over for. Not to fight or fly airplanes, but to make the food. He was very good at it, but the students made fun of him. I came to visit him once. I saw the way they looked at his leg. They mocked him in low voices over by the ovens.

I hated them for it. I waited in the corner until the class had finished, and then as they walked past me to the hallway, I gave Liam a long, lingering kiss in the front of the room.

◆ ◆ ◆

There were nights when I had to work. I wasn't sure what he did on those nights. I knew he had a few friends nearby, other teachers, and he went to the bars with them sometimes. But mostly, I assumed, he stayed home and watched TV.

One afternoon, I left work early to surprise him. It was his birthday, and my mother and I had made him a cake.

He lived in the kind of neighborhood a single man could buy on a teacher's salary—boxy brick houses with little lawns and hedges between the driveways. There were vases and knickknacks behind the windows, like storefronts.

He had asked me to live with him many times. But I knew that if I did that, we wouldn't be waiting anymore for the next good thing. We would get married eventually, but after the wedding I would come home to the breakfast dishes still in the sink. I liked the life we had, when it was still in front of us.

When I turned the corner onto his lane there was a limousine parked out front of his house. Liam came outside with a knapsack over his shoulder.

I got out of my car. "Are you going somewhere?" Right away, I thought he had another woman in the backseat of the car.

"Hon, wait," he said.

His leg was giving him trouble; he had a hard time walking toward me. I threw open the door to the limousine as he limped toward me, but I was too far away. He fell onto the grass, and the driver came out of the car to help him up.

There was no one else in the limousine.

"Tell me what's going on," I said.

Liam held onto the driver's shoulder to steady himself. "It's free. It's a gift."

"A gift from who?"

"From a hotel. In Atlantic City."

"Why would they give you a limousine?"

Liam took a handkerchief out of his pocket and rubbed it across is forehead. "I should have told you," he said. "I'm sorry."

"You've been gambling?"

"I'm sorry," he said again. "I wanted to surprise you."

"Surprise me? With what?"

The driver took off his cap and got back inside the car to wait.

"I've been trying to make enough to buy a restaurant," Liam said. "Then I was going to stop."

"How much have you lost?" I asked him.

He mumbled something.

"What?"

"Twenty thousand."

"Twenty thousand dollars," I said slowly. "Twenty thousand."

"No," he said, his eyes shining. "I've *made* 20,000."

I blinked at him. "Oh," I said after a moment. "Oh."

He took my shoulders in his hands. "Twenty thousand dollars, Liz." He whooped. "Twenty fucking thousand dollars!"

"I know," I said. "It's a lot."

He frowned. "Aren't you happy? Don't you get it? I'm *rich*."

I thought about it. "I *am* happy."

"Well," he said. "You sure aren't acting like it."

I took his hand and tried to smile. "Why don't I go with you this
time?"

◆ ◆ ◆

Liam won $5,000 more that weekend. He showed me around the
casino floor with his chest puffed out and his arm around my waist.
He'd been coming one night a week for two years, and I'd never
known.

He won $7,000 more in the next two months. He left every other
Friday to drive down to the casinos, coming back on Sunday. Before
he came home, he drove to the bank and put all the money away in
a savings account. I kept waiting for him to lose, but if he did, he
never said. He kept his account balance on a little black notebook
that he always had in his back pocket.

◆ ◆ ◆

In September we drove up to Boston for my girlfriend's wedding.
She and I had been roommates our first year in college, and she was
marrying her college sweetheart. They'd met in the student bar when
we were eighteen. I remembered him with pimples, shaving in his
boxers in front of our bathroom mirror. I had thought it probably
wouldn't last.

The reception was in an old theater that had been turned into a
banquet hall. The seats had been removed to make space for the
tables and the dance floor. But the mezzanine was still there, and
the chandeliers and the angels carved into the walls.

Thick white candles burned on the tables; there were triangles of
butter on the edges of every plate. The favors were small chocolate
eggs in blue boxes. The band played jazz music, sitting on folding
chairs set up on the stage, and as they began their second song the
waiters came around holding trays of canapés. The moon came
through the skylight and spilled over the tables, and there was a
little pool of light in the center of the room.

As the music slowed down after the dinner, the bride said she was
going to throw the bouquet. My college friends prodded me in the
side. "You catch it," they told me.

The bride called the unmarried girls together. She went up to the balcony with her flowers and we stood in a cluster on the floor by the stage. My girlfriends pushed me to the front. "Go on, Liz."

I saw Liam sitting with the other men at the tables, waiting and laughing. They watched us struggle to grope our way to the front of the group.

Then unexpectedly, without counting to three, the bride threw the bouquet off the balcony. I saw it falling and reached out for it. It fell into my hands and I don't know why, but I was startled. I dropped it. It all happened as if in slow motion. Another girl threw herself onto the floor to grab it.

I looked over at Liam. He wasn't smiling anymore. I had this terrible, gut-deep feeling of having let him down. But for the first time, getting married didn't seem so bad. If I left him, I knew someone else would marry him for the money. I would marry him in spite of it. Because he was a good man. Because there was a difference between being a bad person and just being a lucky one.

Rachel's Story

She comes to my window like this almost every night, tapping her fingers on the glass. *Let me in.* She is always laughing. *Come on, Matty, open the window.* In the dark, her eyes are bright as lanterns. I want to tell her to stop doing this, it can't be good. But somehow I can't bring myself to say it. I'd hate for her to go. If she goes now, she won't come back again.

◆ ◆ ◆

She graduated in a white gown with her arms full of roses, me on her right and Bobby on her left. We had the same last name, all three of us, which would have been exceptional if not for the fact that our shared name was Russo, common among Italian American people. We met during registration in the fall of freshman year, under the violent lights of a damp, custard-colored classroom.

Rachel was not especially beautiful, but she had the scent of someone beautiful—a kind of clean, wet-grass smell. It was the kind of smell that reminded you of summer camp, of sitting by the lake at night with your arm around a girl. She was fresh, part of the earth and the natural state of things. Originally from Oregon, she had moved to Colts Neck, New Jersey when she was fifteen, where her father was stationed at the Naval Weapons Station. She therefore lacked the common native artificialities—the acrylic nails and highlights and colored contact lenses—that characterized the girls I had dated in high school. After I came to know her, it seemed I could not remember a time in my life when Rachel had *not* been there.

She was a tiny thing, not even five feet tall, and she often wore baggy sweaters with huge, draping sleeves. Her long hair was so blond it was white, which was rare for an Italian girl, and she was pretty in a petite, interesting kind of way, like the girl who plays the best friend in movies, but can never be the star. From her mother she had inherited a thin, beaklike nose and a broad, square face, which she would remind me, every other day or so, that she hated. She had grown up as a military brat, moving eight times before she went to college, and she wasn't afraid of much.

She did not realize that I loved her. "You know, Matty," she joked once, throwing her arm in its heavy sleeve around my elbow and resting her pink face on my shoulder, "I'm glad we'll never date. I like you too much to do that to you."

Since the first day of freshman year, she and Bobby and I were best friends. We went to meals together and joined the intramural soccer team and the college theater group. It began as a platonic friendship. Once, during a spring break trip to Florida, the three of us passed out on the same hotel bed, drunk as lords. But it never went any farther than that until our senior year at Rutgers, when Rachel asked Bobby out for lunch alone.

The meal was a betrayal I could never quite forgive. They began to date exclusively after that, and although we remained friends, they were alone together more than they were with me. They began to share beds, meals, and jokes I was not privy to, and I tried to find for myself the happiness Rachel had found with him. I started sleeping around, but the only one I ever saw in bed with me was her.

I suspected she'd been in love with Bobby from the start. He had those tragic Bob Dylan eyes, and with his thick black hair he was handsomer than she was pretty, and I could tell she felt lucky to be with him. But why Bobby decided to date her, and whether he ever really loved her at all, was a mystery to me. He'd been with plenty of girls over the years, and they were all much prettier than Rachel. After a while I figured that, in the end, being with her was just *easier*—she was sweet, and comfortable, and she loved him. They laughed and got high together.

But I'm not going to say that's *all* there was to it. I like to think he loved the same things about her that I did—her dark smiling eyes, and the spirit in her, the way she squealed when she opened a gift.

Throughout our college years, Bobby had his heart set on moving to LA and becoming an actor. Rachel wanted to go with him, of course, and I wanted to be with her, so after graduation we rented a

U-Haul and drove I-80 across the country. When we got to California, Rachel moved into her cousin's rented apartment on San Fernando Road, and Bobby and I found a shabby, ground-floor apartment three blocks away.

It was very small, and it was located on an intersection, so that at night the headlights of cars would sweep through our bedrooms like ghosts. Despite these shortcomings, however, Rachel desperately wanted to live there with us. The possibility of cohabitation—of graduating into a "grown-up" relationship with Bobby—thrilled her. She made her case to Bobby, but he said he wanted to focus on his career first, and when he started making some money they could find a place of their own.

Rachel pouted for a while, but eventually backed off. She found a job in a bakery that made wedding cakes. She did supply inventories and gave out cake samples in little paper cups. Bobby and I bartended in a pizzeria two blocks away, and before our shift we would come into the bakery to see Rachel, whose shift was just ending. Bobby would talk about the auditions he had gone to that day, and Rachel would ask me about the actress-waitresses at the restaurant. She'd say, "Did you get any numbers yet, hotshot?" and I would laugh and say, "I'm working on it," and I would wonder whether sleeping with other girls would make her jealous. But I worried that if it didn't bother her, I wouldn't be able to bear it, and in the end I stayed single.

It seemed Rachel and I were just about the only people in Hollywood who *didn't* want to be actors. The truth was, though, neither of us knew what we wanted. In college I had majored in classics, and Rachel in sociology, but by our senior year we were both so bored it was all we could do to make it through the classes. I knew Rachel liked to take pictures, and sometimes she talked about taking a trip with her mother to New York to see some of the galleries. But whether it was about money, or the possibility of Bobby's infidelity, or something else, she never went.

◆ ◆ ◆

So we'd been together four years, Bobby and Rachel and me. But things started to fall apart the summer after we moved to Hollywood, when we were driving from LA to Angel Stadium in the green

Ford truck Bobby had bought from Rachel's cousin. Bobby was at the wheel. We were speeding down the highway with the windows open, and Rachel was snapping photos from the front seat with her old camera.

So right there, that's Rachel in the front next to Bobby, and me in the backseat behind her. She's got a big hardbound book on her lap, full of black-and-white portraits of celebrities. That's because we're doing this thing we always used to do on road trips to pass the time, taking turns reading to each other. We also took turns choosing the book, and we'd gone through three Harry Potters this way, and one book of Langston Hughes's poems. And after a while it became like a good-luck kind of thing, like if we *didn't* read in the car we'd all be doomed or something. So we started reading everywhere, even for ten-minute drives.

But on this particular afternoon Rachel pulls out this picture book with all the celebrities, and it doesn't take long for Bobby and I to realize there's not a single word in that book past the copyright page. Bobby leans over. "What the hell?"

Rachel shrugs. "I liked it. I'll just make up the story to go with the pictures."

I press my face to the window. "Is there a bookstore around here? Bobby, stop when you see a bookstore, will you?"

"Does it look like there's a bookstore around here?"

"Well, then just stop on the side. We can leave Rachel there."

Rachel reaches behind her and swings her bag at me.

We all laugh, but neither Bobby nor I want to admit that we are genuinely worried that Rachel's mistake may have brought catastrophe upon us. Bobby's hands tighten around the steering wheel. He speeds up.

"Hey, pull over," I say. "I gotta piss."

But Bobby only presses the gas harder.

"Come on, turn off here, what are you doing?"

Rachel grabs his leg. "Come on, slow down."

He looks over at her, then back at me. Seeing our faces, so serious and afraid, he opens his mouth and begins to howl with laughter. "Guys, guys," he says finally, "I'm kidding." He takes his foot off the gas.

From my seat, I can see his foot moving toward the brake pedal. But he's still looking at Rachel, and suddenly the car in front of us brakes too, fast and hard. Rachel cries out, she grabs the wheel and yanks it toward her to avoid the car, and Bobby flings his hands in the air. Our truck spins off the highway, through the guardrail and down the hill. Rachel is screaming, I can hear her but I can't do anything except watch the clouds sliding like pucks across the sky.

◆ ◆ ◆

When I wake up, red siren lights are spinning above my head. Rachel and Bobby are sitting on the grass next to me.

"He's awake!" Rachel reaches out to touch me, but someone else is there and blocks her hand. "Don't touch," they say.

I blink at her. The rims of her eyes are red. "It's okay now," she assures me, but her voice is trembling. "You're okay."

I try to sit up but am forced back down again. "Let me up," I say. "I feel fine."

"They won't let us come with you," she says. "So my cousin's coming to take Bobby and me home, okay? But I'll come over to the hospital as soon as I'm allowed."

Bobby taps the side of the stretcher. "Stay strong, my man. Do you want me to call your mom?"

"No! If she calls, tell her I'm working late." I struggle to sit up. I don't see why I have to go the hospital, strapped onto a cot like an invalid.

As they lift my stretcher into the ambulance, I see Rachel and Bobby bent toward each other. They are completely absorbed in their survival. Their foreheads are touching. He puts his hand on her cheek. I imagine he is telling her, for the first time, that he loves her, and I want to scream that he doesn't know the first thing about loving her, but the ambulance doors close and I am apart from them again.

◆ ◆ ◆

Rachel comes to pick me up in her cousin's cherry-red convertible, her hair pulled back into a ponytail. When she throws her arms around me, she holds the back of my head with her palm. "I knew they wouldn't find anything wrong with you! Didn't I tell you?"

The floor of the car is dirty, littered with cigarette stubs. When she sees me looking at them she says, "It's gross, I know, try not to look. It's not my car." She sighs, searching her purse for the keys. "I don't know what Bobby's gonna do about the Ford. The hood's busted and it'll take at least a week to fix." She looks up at me. "So how are you feeling? Are you okay?"

I laugh, shrugging off her question. "It was just a concussion."

She smiles. "I knew you'd be okay. I've always thought you were invincible, and I guess I was right." She adjusts the rearview mirror and sighs heavily. "Now that we're all okay, it kind of feels like magic, though, don't you think? It's kind of like—I don't know, like being reborn. Like we're being given a second chance." She reaches toward me. For a second I think she's going to hold my hand. But instead she dips her fingers into the console, where her lip balm is buried under a pack of tissues. She glances in the mirror as she puts it on. "This whole thing is like a dream. I can't believe it even happened. Bobby's been acting really nice all day, really attentive and everything." She smiles. "And he wants to take me out to dinner tonight. . . ." She hesitates, biting her lip. "Are you mad? I don't want to leave you after all that's happened. . . We can all go together if you want."

I laugh a little. "What? No, you guys should go. It's not like I've had some big surgery or anything. I've been in the hospital for like, two hours."

"Are you sure?"

"Of course."

"Thanks, Matty."

I don't say anything more, and Rachel says, "You're still in shock about everything, aren't you? I can see it in your face." Then she really does take my hand. I can't remember the last time she touched me. "It's okay to be scared," she tells me softly.

◆ ◆ ◆

When we arrive at the apartment the sun has gone down. Rachel throws open the door and announces me: "And so he arrives, the Great Mateo!" I roll my eyes, and she says, "Nah, I'm only kidding. Everything's fine. There's nothing wrong with him." I'm glad she isn't making a big deal about my concussion, especially in front of Bobby.

Bobby comes over and takes my elbow, clapping my back with his right hand. "Hey, man. I'm glad you're okay."

"Thanks." I can see Rachel out of the corner of my eye, fussing with her hair clip that's just fallen out. "So," I say. "You guys are going out?"

Bobby looks at Rachel. "Can I talk to you?"

"Oh," she says, surprised. "Okay." He leads her into the kitchen.

I can hear them arguing in muffled tones. "But you promised," she is saying, close to tears. "How can you go to an audition? We almost died together."

"Yeah, but carpe diem, right? Don't be mad. This audition is *huge*, babe, and I only just found out about it."

When she doesn't respond, I imagine he pulls her closer and moves his hand through her hair. "Hey," he tells her. "We'll do it tomorrow night, okay? Same plan. Just tomorrow."

"Tomorrow is too late," she says. "It won't feel the same tomorrow. We were lucky *today*. It was supposed to be the start of something."

"It still is."

"This is about that waitress, isn't it? That stupid one, what's her name, Diana? Are you seeing her tonight?"

Bobby laughs. "Seriously? Now you're just being fucking crazy."

When they emerge, Rachel is holding her bottom lip between her teeth, but when she sees me staring she flashes a forced smile and flops down on the couch across from me. Bobby sits down next to her and puts his arm around her shoulder. We sit there quietly for a while, none of us wanting to be the first to speak.

Rachel finally breaks the silence. "You know," she says brightly, picking at a thread on the throw pillow. "I think we should buy a puppy."

"Jesus, Rach." Bobby rolls his eyes. "What does that have to do with anything?"

"I was thinking about it while I was driving Matty home. And if you're not gonna celebrate our survival by taking me to dinner, I think we should get a dog." She turns to me. "Don't you think so, Matty?"

"Hey." I put my hands in the air. "Leave me out of this."

I've offended her, though. "You don't have to say it like *that*," she says. "It could be your dog too. You live here, you'd have to help with it."

"But *you* don't live here," Bobby says.

Rachel winces. "Well, we could share him. Like, you get him on weekends."

"Like a divorced couple splitting a kid?" He laughs.

"Well, something like that. It doesn't matter anyway. I'm here all the time. I could just move in."

Bobby stands up then and sighs. "Let's talk about this later. I'm gonna go get us some food."

"You can't just walk away like that!" Rachel screams as he moves toward the door. She throws a shoe at him. It hits him on the back of the shoulder, but he doesn't turn around.

"Don't worry about him," I tell her when he's gone. "He's just freaked out by what happened. He wants to forget it. I'm sure he just feels guilty because he was the one driving."

"But I don't *want* to forget it." She pouts. "Where's my bag?" When she finds it, she pulls out a joint and goes out to the patio.

I follow her. "What are you doing?"

"Want some?" She holds it out to me.

I grab her wrist. She looks up at me, surprised. "I thought you stopped doing that after college."

"I did stop. It's Bobby's." She twists out of my grip, then sighs and throws the joint on the ground. "Oh, forget it," she says, but I'm not sure she's talking to me. "What a fucking waste of my time."

♦ ♦ ♦

October: still no puppy, none of Rachel's boxes stacked on our living room floor. Her cousin has moved back to Oregon, and Rachel is in between roommates now, living alone. She is quieter, more thoughtful than she was when we first moved here. She says she has rediscovered the Catholicism of her childhood, although in college she explored Islam and Judaism and her interest seems more like another fad than a reclamation of her faith.

Still, I see her praying in the kitchen on the mornings when she has spent the night here. She bends over the counter in the early light, counting beads.

This is Rachel, waiting for Bobby to wake up one morning and tell her how he's been a fool, how all along his happiness has been in her. Once, on one of those rare occasions when I go over to her house without him, I find a tattered copy of *Modern Bride* stuffed between her toilet and the bathtub. I'm surprised by how careless she is about hiding it, until I realize she has left it there on purpose. She wants me to tell Bobby. She is using me as a messenger.

I know it's not really about a wedding for her. It's a statement of protest, a way to let him know he's being unfair by not letting her move in, especially when she's paying an entire apartment's rent now. But I have no intention of telling Bobby. I am certain this discovery will unhinge him, frighten him into doing something drastic. And if they split up, Rachel will move back to New Jersey, and this means I will lose her.

I can't lose her.

Sometimes when we all get drunk together and Bobby's at the bar or in the bathroom, I think about saying to her, "Did you ever wonder about going away together, you and me? For good? We could go anywhere."

I feel light as paper. The music is pounding, and her face is strobe lit. I'm certain she'll say yes. And then we could just blow away, Rachel and me. I could gather her up and we would float away, away from the painted faces of LA and the stink of booze on the street and into the night.

But then Bobby returns. She nuzzles his shoulder gently with her nose, and Bobby turns and looks at her with such tenderness that for a second I can see how it is that she loves him. And I wonder, if she loves him so much for these rare moments, wouldn't she love me a hundred times more? I reach out and touch her back with my hand. She turns, startled. I have broken her moment. "What is it, Matty?"

"No, nothing," I say quickly. "Sorry."

◆ ◆ ◆

This is the last day. Wednesday, the day before Thanksgiving. We have decided to stay in LA, and are planning a barbecue in Rachel's backyard with a few of our friends from work.

This is Bobby and me, sitting by the pool, the sun ignited. "Fuckin' beautiful California!" we marvel, every day that week. "November and warm as shit!" But Rachel doesn't seem as thrilled by the weather. I think she's a little unsettled by the warmth. It is the first Thanksgiving she will have spent this way—palm trees instead of snow, and paper plates and a chipped red picnic table.

This night is the first in a while that she doesn't come over; she's been cooking all day, and calls Bobby at 8 to tell him she's falling asleep. From my bedroom, I hear the murmurs of their good night.

Later Bobby and I drink beer together. Bored, we flip through the channels five times over until we settle for reruns of *Home Improvement.*

"Does Rachel seem upset to you?" I ask him.

Bobby shrugs. "She just misses her mom. She'll be fine." He opens his seventh beer, and I wonder if he's drinking more than he usually does because, although he won't admit it, he's worried about her.

"You think we should go over there?"

"Nah." He shakes his head. "She's sleeping." He looks at me strangely. "Why?"

We rarely talk about their relationship. For all the hours we spend together, I realize, we've never talked about very much at all.

"Nothing," I say. "It was just a thought."

I think how superficial our friendship has been. All this time, it's always been about Rachel.

We keep drinking. By his tenth beer, Bobby is slurring his words. Before long he's piss drunk, and he's doing the Tim Allen *har-har-har* all around the apartment. I'm cheering him on, and we're both laughing, having a good though superficial time. And then, very suddenly, he stops and stares at me, his eyes narrowed. "You stay away from her," he says, reaching out for me. "She's *mine!*"

And then—bam! He falls onto the couch, passed out.

I take off his shoes and cover him with a blanket. Then I turn off all the lights and go into my bedroom.

◆ ◆ ◆

That night I am woken at midnight by the sound of glass shattering in our living room. At first I think it is Bobby, stumbling his way to bed. Then I hear a voice I can't place.

Someone has broken into our apartment, I realize. I grab my cell phone and the heaviest object I can find, my desk lamp. Trembling, I sneak into the hallway.

That's when I see Bobby, upright on the sofa. In front of him, amid the remnants of our glass coffee table, is Diana, the waitress from the pizzeria. She's drunk, swaying dangerously, about to fall onto the hundreds of tiny glass shards of the table she broke only moments before.

"Bobby, catch her!" I shout at him from the doorway. He turns his head toward me slowly, confused, but he is still too far gone to understand what is happening.

Diana is toppling fast, and as she collapses I find myself diving and reaching for her waist, sliding into the glass. It feels like the pain of a thousand knives in my knees.

Diana squirms out of my grip and looks over at me, grinning. "Matt? Is that you? Heeey, Matt! How's it goin'?"

Bobby is still sitting on the sofa, immobile. He shakes his head hard, like a pony. "Sorry . . . sorry . . ." he says. "Dude. I'm fucking wasted."

I stand up and examine my legs. I can count five or six tiny pieces of glass in the skin, which is not as bad as I thought, but it still hurts like hell.

Diana falls onto the couch next to Bobby. She waves at me to come closer. "I walked. Here," she slurs. "From the bar. At the corner. I came to see. Bobby." She presses her mouth against my ear. Despite the pain in my knees, I catch my breath at the touch of her lips. "I have a *crush* on him," she whispers, louder than she means to, and laughs hysterically.

Maybe I should help them. Get them water, make them eat pretzels and swallow Tylenol. Call a taxi to take Diana home. But why? She doesn't want me, and Rachel doesn't want me, and I am dizzy and tired, and there is blood on the carpet. They are already fast asleep on the sofa, drunk and dream-struck, their faces swollen as pumpkins from the alcohol. It is all I can do just to lock the door, pick the glass out of my legs, and crash into a painful, lonely, sleep, leaving them passed out there together.

♦ ♦ ♦

And when Rachel arrives at my window later that night, tapping her fingers on the glass—*Matty, let me in*—I know I should tell her to go home. A good man, I know, would shake his head and tell her to go, would not want her to walk into the living room and see Diana and be hurt in this way. A good man would put his hand to his forehead and say, "Oh, no, Rach, we drank waaay too much tonight. Bob's not in good shape."

But I do not want to be a good man. I want her to see Bobby at his worst, to realize who she's been giving herself to, night after night. When I open my eyes and see her standing on the lawn outside my bedroom, tapping, I stumble toward her in my boxers and open the window.

She climbs inside. "I'm sorry," she says, "I couldn't sleep, I got lonely. I tried to call Bobby but he's not answering his phone."

I nod.

She looks at me suspiciously. "But he is here, isn't he?"

"Yeah," I say. "He's here."

She looks down at my knees, caked with spots of dried blood, and gasps. "What happened to your legs?"

I open my bedroom door and lead her into the living room. The first thing she sees is the floor, covered in glass. Then she sees Bobby and Diana, their bodies woven together on the couch.

Rachel puts her hand to her mouth. She stares at them for a long time. Then she turns to me, tears streaming down her face. "How could you not tell me before this? How could you let me find out this way?"

Her accusation startles me. She is supposed to be angry with Bobby, not with me. Now is the time for her to say, Let's get out of here, okay, Matty? Let's move back to the East Coast together and start over.

But she doesn't. Instead she is sick with sorrow for him, for what she has lost.

She runs to the front door and pulls at the lock, trying to open it.

"Wait," I say. "Don't go like this, please. Why don't we go get a drink or something? We can talk about it."

She looks at me like I'm crazy. "I don't want to *drink* right now, Matt."

"It doesn't have to be alcohol. We can drink coffee."

She stops pulling at the door. "Are you asking me to go *out* with you? Like this?"

I'm trembling. "He doesn't deserve you, Rachel."

She shakes her head. And before I can say anything else, she is gone.

◆ ◆ ◆

The next morning her clothes were gone from her apartment. She had closed her email account and left her cell phone behind. She left nothing else but one of Bobby's T-shirts and a couple of empty journals. Bobby never learned what had happened that night. I expected him to take it in stride, shrug it off and forget about her. But to my surprise, he walked around for days in a haze, saying he didn't understand, asking me if I'd heard from her.

I said no, no I hadn't. Some days he was furious with her. Others he was worried. He said what if something bad had happened to her. I had to tell him: she's taken all her things with her, obviously she's just left. He was constantly sweating. The extent of his grief unnerved me; I realized I had never really known him at all.

I had not expected Rachel to leave the way she did. She had always been afraid of confrontation, but I never thought she would leave without saying goodbye. I thought there must have been more to it. She must have been falling out of love with Bobby already, all that time. Every canceled date, every look of disdain had broken a little piece of her until very little remained of the Rachel she used to know. She left, I thought, to build herself again.

A few months went by with no word from her. Bobby and I called her mother's house in New Jersey, but no one answered.

Not long afterward, Bobby landed a spot on a television pilot. The pilot was picked up for the season, and he started spending more and more time at the clubs with the cast members. One day he came home from work and asked me if one of his cast mates could have my bedroom. That's when I left too.

Not long after I returned to New Jersey, I got a letter from Rachel in the mail, sent to my parents' house: "To Matty," it said, "c/o Mrs. Russo." It was printed on stationery that said Holiday Inn, Santa Fe. Enclosed was a photo of her with her arm around a huge white dog. They had the same blue-gray eyes. She looked happy.

Wrapped around the photo, her note said, *He's not mine. I borrowed him for the picture. But I might keep him. Miss you. R.*

In this way, she forgave me. Over the next year she sent me postcards every month or so. She got older in those cards. I imagined that when she was a child moving from base to base, she had never gone to a new place by choice. Her parents had chosen her college; Bobby had chosen LA. For the first time, she was free to choose her own life, and do as she pleased.

She drifted farther east with each postcard: Kansas City, Chicago, Birmingham. She was always very careful not to give away anything that would allow me to find her or write back to her. Then she said she found a job working for some newspaper in Pennsylvania, and I got excited, starting thinking we would be able to meet. But after that, the postcards stopped coming. I tried to find her. One afternoon I called ninety-eight Russos in the Philadelphia area and as many newspapers as I could find. But no one had heard of her. It was if she had disappeared completely.

After a while I found a job doing special events for a casino in Atlantic City. The work kept me busy, but every night when I went to sleep, under the colored lights of the city, I thought about her. Some nights I was worried; others, hurt. But mostly I was angry. I imagined what I'd say to Rachel if I ever saw her again. I wanted to shake her, demand answers. But I knew all I'd really say was, "What did I ever do to you but love you?" And I hated myself for it.

+ + +

A year after I moved to Atlantic City, my father had knee surgery and was confined to a wheelchair. I spent a week in Morristown with him and my mother, and not long after I went back to my apartment and started work again, I started seeing Rachel outside my window at night. *Matty,* she'd say. *Let me in.* She would tap on the window, her eyes not gray like they'd always been but ice blue. I wanted to open the window, but I was afraid she had only come to say goodbye. "I can't, Rachel," I would tell her. "Look what happened the last time I let you in. You left me."

Then she'd pout at me. "But I came back, Matty. See?"

"Tell me where to find you," I said, "and I'll come to you." But she only laughed.

It got so bad I went to the doctor and asked for pills. The first night I downed two of them with a glass of water. Five minutes later I was drifting into sleep. But just as I'd crossed over into dreaming—the voices from my radio faraway and swooning, old friends waving from the other side—my cell phone rang. I recognized the area code, and at first I thought it was my aunt, calling about my father.

But when I answered, there was a different voice on the other end of the line, one I barely recognized. I hadn't heard it in years.

"Matt? It's Fae. Rachel's mom."

"Mrs. Russo?" My words came out slurred because of the medicine.

"It's about Rachel," she said. Right off the bat. Just like that.

It happened on a Greyhound bus outside Pittsburgh two days earlier. A truck crashed through the divider on I-80, and it was all very quick; she didn't suffer. There would be a memorial service.

"She always talked about you," her mother told me. "She talked about you all the time, even after she left California."

There was so much I wanted to ask her. I had the sense there were two Rachels—the first one, the one I knew, and the person she later became. I wanted to ask her mother, had she dyed her hair or started smoking again or found a boyfriend? I wanted to say didn't she realize that Rachel had died because she left California, and she had left California because of me.

I realized that in some ways, after Rachel left, I had still been living with her. I lived in the knowing she was out there somewhere, imagining that she still liked the same things she always had—Chinese food, and Monopoly, and Michael Jackson.

But I never got to ask. The phone fell onto the floor, and my eyes were closing, and the pills overtook me.

In my dreams, I saw Rachel lying in the rubble, alone.

That night and the next, by the window and in my sleep, I waited for her. I wanted to tell her, *If I had been there, at the accident, I would have stayed with you so you weren't afraid. I would have said, Oh, Rach, it's like magic, it's like being reborn. There is nothing scary about it. I would have held your hand, and walked you across the road.*

But Rachel never came.

What Happened On Crystal Mountain

They were living then in Milton, Florida, in a white two-bedroom house outside Whiting Field Naval Base. They were engaged to be married two months later in New York, a large Catholic wedding in a church on Fifth Avenue. There would be a ten-piece orchestra and a four-tiered cake she and Mark had picked out together.

But until then they lived just outside the airfield, at the end of a long and empty stretch of road in the Florida Panhandle. Floribama, they called it. Not the palm trees and white beaches of Miami, just dirt and swamps and auto shops.

Things had been tense between them lately. They had argued again that night. Anne had just finished college and moved in for good a few weeks earlier, but before that they had never lived in the same city, never mind the same house. She had been waiting so many years, it seemed, for the things she imagined came with living together—lazy Sunday mornings, champagne on weeknights, barbeques on the deck.

But when she came for good it wasn't like she had imagined. With his aircraft selection date only a few weeks away, Mark was distant and irritable. He studied twelve hours a day or more, practicing in the simulator late into the night and buried in his books all morning.

He had wanted, she knew, to fly jets since he was a child. It was a boy's dream that began with *Top Gun* and grew, over time, into a man's sense of duty and pride. "I don't want to be flying some mail plane off the side of a ship," he would say. "I want to be *in it*."

And then, a week after she moved in, she missed her period. She knew she couldn't tell Mark, when he was already so anxious. And she was too embarrassed to tell her parents, who had sent her to an expensive Catholic grade school in Brooklyn and an elite private school after that. They wouldn't be angry with her—they weren't naïve enough to think she was a virgin after so many years, even if she was Catholic. But they would be disappointed, and that was worse than anger.

She had been fitted for her wedding gown already and worried it would be too tight, that it would show something during the wedding. But she decided to wait until afterward to tell anyone, when she might get away with pretending it had happened on the honeymoon.

She and Mark fought that night over details of the wedding she couldn't remember later—linen colors or that sort of thing. "You figure it out," he said. "I don't have time for this right now."

"Is it always going to be like this?" She was close to tears. But he went into the extra bedroom so he could study, and eventually he went to bed and she went into the living room and fell asleep.

Then the tapping started.

At first she thought it was coming from inside the house, or inside the house in her dream. But when she opened her eyes she could see a dark figure outside, peering through the front window.

She thought of the look on her parents' faces, fifteen years before, when a police officer came to tell them that her older sister's apartment had been burglarized and she was missing. Her sister was nineteen, but Anne was only six, and didn't really understand. Her father put up fliers and spoke on the news and her mother sat on the floor for hours, cradling her sister's childhood toys. Anne managed to hide one away for herself, a little figurine of a boy banging on a white drum.

But then, two weeks later, her sister came back. She was alive, but she had been very badly hurt. Her body was raw with bruises, and she was never able to smile or laugh the way she had before. She moved home again and took back the bed she had slept in when she was a little girl, in the room next to Anne's, and stayed there until she was thirty and married. When some time had passed since the kidnapping, when Anne was a teenager and they would argue about something, Anne would imagine what it would have been like if her sister had not come back at all, and she would tell her so and then lie awake at night holding the doll she'd saved, wondering how she could have said that kind of thing out loud.

Lying there on the couch in Mark's house, the black figure peering at her through the window, Anne wondered if life had circled back around again, and it was her turn now. She slid off the couch and ran into the bedroom. "Mart." She shook him by the shoulder. "There's someone outside."

Woken from a deep sleep, he gasped and sat up. "What is it?"

"I don't know. Someone's out there."

He sat up and pulled on his jeans. She followed him into the hallway, ready with the phone, and stood a little behind him.

Mark turned on the light outside, and the porch was illuminated. Anne could make out Shep's strong jawline in the light. He held his hand over his eyes, startled by the sudden brightness.

Anne laughed, relieved. "Oh," she said. "It's just Shep." Then she realized that something bad still must have happened for Shep to be here in the middle of the night.

Mark opened the door and rubbed his cheek with his hand. "Jesus, man. You scared the shit out of Anne. She thought you were some kind of kook or something."

But Shep didn't look at her. "You turned your phone off," he said to Mark. "I kept getting your voicemail, and I saw her sleeping in there. . . . I was trying to wake her up without banging the door down." She wondered whether, seeing her on the couch, he had guessed about her fight with Mark.

"It's the middle of the night," Mark said. "What's going on?"

"Someone from our squadron crashed tonight."

Mark put a fist to his mouth, biting the points of his knuckles, and drew in his breath.

"The system's been down since 10," Shep said. "I was trying to check the flight schedule, and then I got a call from Brett saying there'd been a crash, two guys from Four, both fatalities. They won't say who it was, though. Not until they tell the families. There's a whole bunch of guys calling around about it."

"Where did it happen?"

"Crystal Mountain. Just a couple hours ago."

She and Mark had gone hiking there once. "I fly this way sometimes," he'd told her. "Like this, up to Birmingham." He drew a line with his finger across the sky.

"Do you know who was flying tonight?" Shep asked.

Mark looked at the ground, rubbing his eyes. "I don't—no, I don't know."

"Dave?"

"No, I talked to him earlier. He was going out to the bar. Wait. Fuck. O'Neill."

"No, he's home. I just called him. He thought it was you, man. That's why I came over."

Mark looked up then, his face so white Anne could see the veins under his skin. She saw Shep looking at her and felt uncomfortable. Shep was the first secret she had kept from Mark; her pregnancy was the second.

"Miller," Mark said, so quietly Anne could barely hear him.

"What?"

"It was Miller."

"No, man." Shep shook his head. "Yesterday, he said he was driving down to Pensacola today to see some girl."

"Well, he must have been put in the schedule last minute. I saw him in the ready room before my flight. He said he was going out with Roberts on a cross-country."

"Nah," Shep said. "Roberts? No way."

"Who is Miller?" Anne blurted. They both looked at her, surprised, it seemed, to see her still standing there.

"Nick Miller," Mark said. "You know him. He lives down the street."

She remembered him then. He lived with his wife a block down the road. His wife liked to sit on the porch stairs and read books. She was just a few years older than Anne.

Mark had only spoken about Nick Miller once. He had come home all riled up one day, saying that this friend of Shep's kept bragging about being certain he would be selected for fighter jets and not helos, that his aunt and the base commander knew each other from high school and had dated for a while.

Anne left the porch with Mark and Shep and walked toward Nick's house. There was no light except for the moon. As they turned the corner, they could see two Navy police cars parked out front. Shep bent over, putting his hands on his knees, and cried.

◆ ◆ ◆

When Shep left around midnight, she and Mark couldn't sleep. After a while Mark got up and walked circles in the bedroom.

Anne sat on the bed and said she was sorry about fighting with him.

"It's okay." He shrugged. "I'm sorry too."

"How are you feeling about all this?"

He lay down on the bed and put his hand to his forehead. "This is gonna sound crazy, Anne, but I think I heard him. Before he went down."

"You heard who?"

"Nick."

She thought of the man who had called after her sister disappeared, saying he'd seen her in the passenger seat of a car at the gas station. The police spent a week searching the town. When her sister came home a week later, they found out she had been a hundred miles from that gas station at the time. The phone call had been a hoax.

"You're just upset—" she said.

"*No.*" Mark punched his fist into the pillow. "Before I landed, when the sun was going down, I was out there doing my solo flight and I heard something on the radio. I couldn't make it out at first. There was all this static, and I thought I was hearing things."

"What was it?"

He sighed. "It was Nick, I'm sure of it. He was saying, *There's something down there,* or something like that."

"What would be down there?"

"How the hell should I know?"

"Hey," Anne said gently. "It's okay. I'm sure it was something else."

She put her hand on his arm, and he turned to her then with surprise—suspicion, even—like she wasn't even supposed to be there. "You don't know."

"Yeah," she said, and sighed. She had no patience for ghosts anymore. "I guess I don't."

◆ ◆ ◆

Mark liked to talk about life on the carrier. He'd spent a month on the *John C. Stennis* during his time at the Academy, working with the firefighting team. He talked a lot about the fighter pilots he met there, a kind of reverence in his tone. "The thing is," he said, "everyone's there because of them. Three thousand guys on a ship, and they're all making sure these thirty guys can do their job."

He told her a story once—how he followed a trail of blood and found a body on the ship, in the far back end of the bottom deck. The guy wasn't dead yet. An iron hatch had swung loose, hit him on the head, and he had crawled, barely conscious, toward the bathroom.

It was four years into their relationship—just after they'd gotten engaged—when he told her this.

"So you saved this guy's life," she said.

He shrugged. "Nah. Someone else probably would have found him."

She thought she understood then what it must have been like for him—that longing to be back there. It wasn't about being special. It was about being a part of something, fitting in with people who had done extraordinary things. It was about putting up with everything else—their bedroom fights, the late nights of training—until he could get back to that ship.

◆ ◆ ◆

When Mark woke her up the next morning, he was sitting on the edge of the bed, holding Anne's ring between three fingers. She had taken it off in the shower after their fight.

"Marry me," he said.

She swatted at him. "We already did this, remember? I said yes. Let me sleep."

"No," he said. "Marry me. Today."

She sat up on her elbows. "Are you serious?"

"You don't know what could happen."

"That's ridiculous. Nothing going to happen to you."

"But if it does. If I do die, they'll give you a helluva lot of money. If we're married."

"I don't care about the money."

"Please," he said.

Anne hesitated. It would be an easy solution to the awful timing of her pregnancy, to cancel the wedding and marry him right then. But she didn't want their marriage to be about a baby, or money, or

Mark's desperation; she wanted it to be a new start between them. "What about New York?" she said. "We've put down all those deposits. Two hundred people are coming."

"We can still do it. We'll go to the courthouse today, just sign some papers, no one will have to know. Then we'll do our real wedding."

"It wouldn't be real, though. It would be like a game, like acting it."

"Please," he said. He sat down next to her on the bed and put his head on her shoulder. His hair still stank from the sweat inside his helmet the day before. She wanted desperately to wash it for him, to get the smells out.

◆ ◆ ◆

She had no job at the time, nothing to do while she was in Milton. The nearest beach was forty minutes away in Pensacola, and sometimes she went there and put a towel on the sand and read books. But mostly, while Mark was training, she sat at his computer and planned the final details of their wedding. She made phone calls and chose the flowers and the appetizer and the band and thought about what it would be like when they were finally married. She would have a job, of course, and maybe once they both felt useful and satisfied with themselves, they would be happy again. After the wedding they would move to a new place and they would buy furniture together. Until then, Mark's house was almost bare—just a mattress and a couch and a desk in three large white rooms.

But every once in a while, on bright, lonely afternoons in the empty house, she would start thinking about Shep again. How he and Mark, who hadn't known each other then, had both asked her out on the same night, four years earlier.

They were all in college at the time, although Mark and Shep were a year ahead of her. Back then, she had grand dreams of studying international law, of bringing refugees from faraway places and sitting down in Washington offices to negotiate new lives for them. She had come down to the Naval Academy from Bowdoin for a conference on foreign affairs, and Mark was the leader of her discussion group.

During lunch, members of the conference were invited to eat in King Hall with the school's mostly male midshipmen. Her pink sweater stood out among the sea of white, and many of the midshipmen stared at her. She found herself suddenly very shy and was thankful when Mark put his arm around her waist and guided her toward a table of their own. But on the last day, when Mark couldn't come, she sat quietly near the windows with some of the other students from the conference. Toward the end of the meal, Shep came and sat down across from her. He introduced himself and asked if he could call her later.

At first, she wondered if he had approached her on a dare. But he called that night, just like he'd promised. She had turned him down because Mark had called first, and afterward she liked to think things had worked out how they were meant to, that she'd hoped all along it would be Mark who called sooner. "I saw you, and I knew," she used to tell him when they were first dating. But the truth was she couldn't remember whether it was like that or not. She had been eighteen, confused and eager for any attention at all.

In the weeks before their wedding, she started thinking about what would have happened if it had been Shep whose call she had answered. She liked to think she'd be in exactly the same place. They were both pilots, after all. They had many of the same friends; they even had the same champagne shade of blond hair. But deep down she knew this logic was desperate and silly. She had been very young when they met, and she was changing so much, so that every night she felt she was a little bit different from the Anne who had woken up that morning. And those changes had compounded and compounded until she could barely recognize herself, never mind the man she had told, as a college freshman, that she would love forever.

Mark never found out she had met Shep at the conference. He always figured they met down in Milton, and it seemed silly to tell him all those years later, especially since she wasn't even sure if Shep remembered. He didn't say anything about it, if he did. On the base four years later, when Mark introduced them, they shook hands and said hello, and that was all.

Sometimes, she thought she understood Mark's anxiety during training. There he was, flying with his friends off the beaches of Florida, buying rounds in the bars at night and sleeping in his soft American bed, and getting paid the same as guys who were flying in much harder conditions. She knew, although it was never spoken out loud, that a lot of the trainees prayed the war wouldn't end before they got there, because even being dead was better than being an outsider, the one who didn't make it over.

One of her friends from high school had joined the Marines a few months after he graduated. He was five-foot-six, skinny, religious, and the best singer she had ever met. He was not the kind of guy she would have taken for a military man. They had become friends during rehearsals for their high school musical.

He was the kind of actor, people used to say, who found his way into their thoughts at odd hours, weeks after the play had closed. He had this charisma no one could match. When he graduated from high school, he took a few classes at a local college, and then one day he went to the recruiting station. He called later to tell her he was leaving for Camp Pendleton. He was never very good at taking tests or writing papers, he said; he was searching for what felt "right."

"I'll see you, Annie," he said, like he always did, before he hung up.

He went over to Iraq. When he came back, he was different, restless. She used to ask, "What happened there?" but he'd just laugh and say, "I found Saddam. Did I forget to tell you?" Once she asked him if he had killed anyone. "What does it matter?" he said. "Would you feel differently about me if I did?"

He kept saying he was getting out, but she knew it was all for show. The truth was, whatever had happened there, he didn't know how to let it go.

Then, the last week of Anne's junior year in college, he was sent over again. "I'll see ya, Annie," he said before he left. But he didn't see her. He did his six months and when he came home he got out of the service all together. She heard he had moved out west somewhere, to Wyoming or Utah. But she didn't know for sure. He changed his phone number, and she never heard from him after that. She looked for him on TV sometimes, but if he had made it out to Hollywood, she never saw him on-screen.

The morning after the crash, people kept calling to see if Mark was okay. The names of the pilots still had not been released, but the newspapers all the way up to Atlanta were reporting it; footage of the crash site was shown on CNN. A safety stand-down was called, which meant there would be no weekend flights, but there wouldn't be a brief until Monday.

Anne dressed in a little white sundress she used to wear in college, and after he had answered all his messages Mark turned his phone off and they drove to the Escambia County Courthouse in Pensacola. It was a beautiful afternoon. It hadn't rained in days, and the sky was blue as glass. As they drove past the big houses on Scenic Highway, she kept thinking, *On the best day in New York, it wouldn't be this nice.* A wedding seemed like the right thing for both of them, she thought, when she considered their situations.

When the trees became thinner and the road opened out onto the beach, Mark pulled into the parking lot of the Winn Dixie and said he wanted to buy her some flowers to carry. He asked if he could pick them out, so she waited in the car, and when he came out he had this great big armful of orange roses, the same flowers he'd brought her on their first date.

"Do you like them?" he asked.

"Not really," she joked. His face fell. She laughed and put her palms on his cheeks. "I'm kidding. I love them!" For a moment she worried he was upset—she'd only been trying to lighten the mood—but then he started laughing too, so that they were both laughing, sitting on the hood of the car by the beach and laughing like they used to, and for a moment Crystal Mountain was just a name on a map.

To celebrate afterward, they bought wine and cheese and went down near the water to have a picnic. It was cool out, and they sat on the sand, watching the ocean churn white and gray as the sun went down.

On the beach, Mark was suddenly quiet. All day he hadn't stopped talking—he kept saying he loved her, he loved her, they'd be so happy, she'd see. And then, now that they were married, it seemed he couldn't think of anything else to say.

"What are you thinking about?" she asked him, pulling the corners of the blanket around her shoulders.

"What?" He looked at her like he'd forgotten she was there. "Oh. I don't know."

"Yeah, right," she said, and laughed a little. "We're married now. You have to tell me."

He broke one of the crackers into pieces and tossed them near the surf for the birds to eat. "I'm just thinking about the accident, I guess."

She pursed her lips. "Like how it could have been you?"

He nodded.

Oh, you don't have to worry about me, he used to joke, when he was selected for the pilot program and Anne first started hearing rumors—she still wasn't sure if it was true—that 10 percent of pilots didn't make it through their careers. *When have I been in the bottom 10 percent of anything?*

"But it wasn't," she said. "It wasn't you."

A pair of birds hopped up to them, looking for more food. "But what if," Mark threw them the last cracker, "it *should* have been me?"

She felt a wave of nausea rise up into her throat, and she turned around and vomited into the sand.

Mark scrambled to his knees and put his hand on her back. "Are you okay?"

She wiped her mouth and waved him away. "I'm fine." She kicked sand to cover it up.

He moved over to a clean patch of sand, away from their blanket, and he motioned for her to sit down next to him. He said, "I did— this terrible thing."

She felt the hairs on her arm stand up. He was about to tell her he had been with someone else, and she thought about the baby, because now she would have to make a decision for both of them. He was looking at her for a response, and she knew he wanted her to ask him, What? What did you do? But she just sat there.

He said, "You're going to hate me."

"You cheated on me," she said.

He gave her a strange look. "What? No, Anne . . ." His voice trailed off. "It's about Nick."

"What about Nick?"

"A few days ago, I started playing these—tricks, I guess. On Nick. I was pissed at him for bragging about his relationship with the CO, and how he would get special treatment and get selected for jets. It wasn't fair. I didn't know what I'd do if he got sent to fighters and I got screwed because of him. So I thought I'd scare him a little. Distract him."

Anne squinted up at him, into the sun. "What does that mean?" she asked, confused. "What did you do?"

"At first..." he said, "Well, I just called him a bunch of times and hung up in the middle of the night."

The next day she would look back and think how different things would have been if his mistake had been being with someone else. *We'd work it out*, she remembered thinking. *People cheat all the time and go on to have very happy marriages with lots of children.* But his new confession made her uneasy.

"Where was I?"

"Asleep. I left the room and called him from the house phone. There's that number you can dial to make the call show up as unavailable, you know..."

"That's so—childish."

"I know it was messed up," he said. "But I've been going insane here, you know? All this waiting, not knowing where the Navy's gonna send me for the next *ten* years of my life. Ten years—do you know what it's like to sign your life away for ten years? They could send me to some cubicle in the middle of Oklahoma if they wanted to, and I'd have to go." He shook his head. "But Nick...he wasn't afraid. He always seemed so fucking calm. It wasn't right." His voice rose a little. "I didn't mean anything by it, Anne. You have to know that. I just wanted to shake him up a little."

She was disgusted, but she didn't quite understand why he was so worked up over something so small, however mean and petty. "So you played a little joke on him. So what?"

"No..." he said. "It's... After the phone call, I went over to his house. I—made some noises outside his window. Shined lights into his bedroom. It was stupid. I just wanted to spook him, you know?"

She felt the blood rush from her face. "So—what happened?"

"He came outside and looked around. I hid in the bushes. He seemed...tired, I guess. A little scared, maybe." Matt's voice broke.

He pursed his lips. "I think he thought. . . . I don't know what he thought."

Anne felt sick. He had become, she realized with horror, the kind of person she despised—the prankster who lied about seeing her sister, or even the man who had taken her and, just to see her reaction, swore he would kill her but then, laughing at her as she cried, had let her go.

The kidnapper had been, as was usually true in those kinds of cases, someone her sister knew, a man who did yard work for her apartment complex. He had locked her in his basement until police started coming around his neighborhood asking questions. After he let her go he left the same day, and the police never found him, which meant Anne's family had to think about him every day and worry he might come back.

"When did this you go over to his house?"

Mark looked away. "Thursday."

"The night before the crash."

"Yeah."

She thought, trembling, about Mark's certainty that he heard Nick talking before he went down, that he had seen something in the fog. She wondered what had really happened above Crystal Mountain. It was more likely, she knew, that there had been a problem with the plane: engine failure or bird strike. Or that the weather had disoriented Nick. But part of her also knew that to pilots, sleep was as valuable as gold. When they were tired or distracted, they were too slow at the controls, they overlooked things and forgot their procedures. Especially new pilots.

"Please," Mark begged. "Don't be mad."

"I just married you," she said, as if she were just then realizing it. "That's why you wanted to get married today, wasn't it? Because you thought that if I found out about this before the wedding, I wouldn't want to marry you. And you didn't know how long you could keep it from me."

He took her hand and brought it to his lips. "No," he said. "I married you because the first day I saw you, I knew you were the one."

When they reached the car, she turned and glanced back at the beach. In three weeks, after his selection, they would be given orders to move somewhere else.

◆ ◆ ◆

When they drove back to Milton, she took Mark to see the chaplain. She told him he had to confess to someone other than her.

It was early evening and the base was almost empty. All flights had been cancelled for the weekend, and only the parking lot between the gym and the church was being used. Men and women walked slowly between the two buildings like lost children.

They parked near the entrance to the church and walked up to the building together. Anne was still wearing the white dress she had been married in.

"What are you gonna do while I'm inside?" Mark asked.

"I'll just wait on the bench out here."

He looked behind him, at the door, then back at her. "So...you'll be here when I get out?"

She hesitated. "Yes," she said.

When he went inside, she sat down on the bench and watched the people on treadmills behind the glass walls of the gym.

After a few minutes she heard something behind her. When she turned around, she saw Shep coming out of the church.

He seemed distracted. He stood in the doorway for a second, holding the door, although no one was behind him.

She stood up and went over to him. There was an awkward silence. "I'm sorry about what happened to your friend," she said finally.

"Thanks," he said. And then, all of a sudden, he started to laugh.

"What is it?" She wondered if she had said something wrong.

Shep shook his head slowly. "That guy was a real son of a bitch." He sat down on the bench, leaning back against the wood. When he saw her confusion he said, "Nick was the good kind of son of a bitch, though. Once, when we were golfing up near his parents' house in Georgia, some guy bet us he could hit a golf ball twenty yards out of someone's mouth. And Nick, he just laid right down on the ground and put a tee between his teeth." He laughed again. "So the guy hit the ball, and it actually went the twenty yards like he said. But three of Nick's teeth were busted. He had to pay $300 to have a dentist put in caps."

Anne smiled, but she wondered why Shep was telling her this.

"But that wasn't the funny thing. The funny thing was, Nick must have told that story a hundred times after that. He couldn't stop talking about the time someone hit a golf ball out of his mouth. That's the kind of guy he was, you know? He was really proud of shit like that."

"Do you miss him?"

Shep shrugged and rubbed the toe of his boot into the ground. "Someday, a while from now, maybe I'll wake up and I won't think about what happened. But Nick would want me to remember stuff like that stupid golf ball thing, and tell it to my kids, and have them tell it to their kids, till so many people know about Nick Miller and the golf ball that I couldn't count them all."

Anne thought she knew what he was trying to say. The thing about ghosts, she had always figured, is that when something bad happened they stayed with you, even when everything turned out all right. By now her sister was married and had two children and a townhouse in Baltimore. But every morning when Anne woke up, she still saw her sister at the foot of the bed, the way Anne imagined she looked when she was taken—nineteen and afraid, in the pink slippers and the nightgown she used to wear on Christmas mornings.

For Shep, there would be a time when he wouldn't think about Nick Miller anymore. But Mark, she thought, would be haunted by it for the rest of his life.

She thought she felt the baby flutter, even though she knew it was way too early for that. "Do you remember," she said, "back at the Academy, when you tried to call me that last night of the conference?"

Shep looked up, surprised. "I didn't think you even knew I called."

She nodded. "I did. But I was out with Mark already."

"Oh," he said. "Yeah, I figured that was it, anyway."

She took a breath. "But now I wonder if. . ."

He was looking at her, waiting for her to continue. He had such brightness about him, such a sense of possibility, and she wanted that, she wanted the ease with which he moved about in the world. But—she realized—she didn't want *him*.

She never finished her sentence. It was the first real decision, she felt, she had made in her life.

"Please, can you take me home?" she asked him. "I can't be here anymore."

As they drove away, she thought of Mark coming out of the church to find the bench empty. She knew he would go out to the parking lot first, thinking she had decided to wait at the car. Then he would look in the gym, and after that, she thought, he would realize she had left. Someone Mark knew might come out of the gym and tell him that he saw her leave with Shep, and Anne wondered what Mark would think then, if she would become one of his ghosts too.

The tough thing about Nick Miller's death, Anne imagined—one of the reasons it was so hard for Mark to come to terms with it—was that every day, when he was up there 30 or 40,000 feet off the ground, it was like he was already halfway to wherever Nick was. Up there, he could *almost* cross over, if he could go high enough, or fast enough.

Eventually, when Mark and the others finished their training, they would pin on their wings and go over to Iraq. But it would be hard, Anne realized, for them to think of Nick somewhere else, watching them go over without him. They would imagine it was the same kind of restlessness, the same kind of wistfulness, that they had had every day in Milton, flying those meaningless training flights over the mountains, just waiting for their chance to get over to the desert. It would be hard for them to think of someone waiting forever.

A week after her courthouse wedding, she moved back to New York. She got a job teaching English in a school down the street from where she grew up. The baby was still her secret, and because of that it felt precious inside her. Sometimes, caught up in the chaos of the city, she thought about the women who had taken her place in Milton, the ones who had moved to the base after she left. She imagined that they waited, just as she had, for someone to come home at night, or not to come home. While their fiancés and boyfriends were flying, they planned weddings and read novels on the porch.

And sometimes they couldn't wait anymore. So they went inside. Or they left.

She read in the paper later that month, when the investigation was complete, that the crash had happened the way everyone had suspected. The engine had failed, and with no ejection seat on the early models of the plane, there was no time to get out.

This is what the newspaper said. But sometimes, she couldn't help wondering what Mark had heard that night on the radio, if it was still possible Nick had actually seen something in the dark that night...the same way she used to see her sister at the foot of her bed.

And, for a long time, she wondered whether Mark still flew over Crystal Mountain every chance he got, hoping to see it too.

Little Angels, Little Dolls

We're sitting around the table on the deck, watching the waves puff their chests like proud men.

My father and I have come to Ocean City, New Jersey from Morristown, as we have every summer since I was born. It is a tradition begun by my grandparents over half a century before. We have rented the house on Third Avenue with his family—my grandmother, my Aunt Sue and her daughter Courtney, five years older than me. Courtney has brought her newborn, Ellie, still red and wrinkled as a prune. The baby reaches for dust and invisible things, smuggling them into her fist.

Grandma folds her hands over her embroidery. She seems relaxed, drugged by the breeze. "Oh, there's a lot I never got to do," she says, stroking the gold band on her finger. She speaks slowly and closes her eyes, like a poet memorizing a line. "I never got to go to Coney Island. All that time living in New York, and I never got to go."

"That's not true, Mom," Aunt Sue says. "You took us to Coney Island when we were little, remember?"

I wish Dad would say something, but I know he won't. Aunt Sue looks away. "It's not a good place anymore, Ma. It's not safe. It isn't the same as it used to be."

My grandparents met at a party in Ventnor in 1934, a shore town that found immortality on the Monopoly board only one year later. Sometimes, on a drive to Atlantic City, we would pass the white Victorian house where the party took place, and Grandma would press her face to the window and say, "That's where we met!" as if telling us for the first time. At their fiftieth anniversary party, I saw photos of her leaning against his arm in the foyer of the house. They were beautiful then. She tilted her head, smiling at the camera; his face was turned into her cheek.

She lost her looks, though, long before I could remember them, and when he died, she lost her memory, too. All those delicate moments gone. Small things, like purses left behind, became birthday cards mailed a month too late, real friends confused with those from books. And though memories of Ocean City—streets names, menu specials, the price of cherries in 1974—stayed the longest, even those have begun to erode. She needs constant care now, and heavy sweaters. For travel of long distances, over fifty feet, she is pushed in a chair, her small, round body like a winded puppy bundled up inside a pram. She can't walk much farther than the beach. No one has ever said it out loud before, but I know that, when she is gone, we won't come back here anymore.

"We'll go to the boardwalk tomorrow night, okay, Ma?" Aunt Sue says. "We'll go on the Ferris wheel and you can see the city."

We are early eaters, but we can hear the sounds of families still dining on the porches of nearby houses. The baby starts to cry. Courtney heaves Ellie's little body over her shoulder and stands up. "I think I'll take her to bed now. Good night, everyone."

"Are you going somewhere?" Grandma says, trying to get out of her chair.

Grandma has always been protective of Courtney. For good reason, I suppose, Grandma loves her the most. Courtney's older sister—the first grandchild—died the same year Courtney was born. So Courtney became the first. Before Courtney's prom, Grandma took her shopping on Fifth Avenue in New York; after the engagement, there was the Vera Wang dress and the silver flatware from Christofle.

But when Grandma forgot about my own senior prom, Dad wouldn't remind her. He offered to take me to Nordstrom at the Short Hills Mall as a consolation. He was so proud of himself. I remember thinking, I should buy something to please him, but in the end we couldn't find anything under $200, and I ordered my dress from the Macy's catalogue.

Three years ago, during the month of Courtney's wedding, Dad and I saw her pushing one of Grandma's silver candlesticks into her purse. It was Easter weekend; we were moving Grandma into her room at the senior care center. I was barely sixteen, and I looked at Dad to see what he would do. But he had pressed his chin to his chest and was reworking his tie. When he looked up again, Courtney had moved into another room. I thought maybe he hadn't seen her after all. But then he held up his hand. "Don't," he said.

On the sidewalk below our balcony, strollers and beach carts rattle over the cracks. Grandma reaches for Courtney's arm. "Don't go," she says.

"We're not leaving," Courtney insists. "We're just going to bed." With her free hand, she pushes a lock of deep red hair behind her ear.

She's a single mother now, with her husband, Bill, in Iraq. She looks a lot like Aunt Sue, and a lot like Grandma when she was young. When I was little, we used to pretend that she was my mother, and for a while, I thought she was. Then she started high school and met Bill, and she stopped being my mother because it occurred to her she could be someone else's one day.

◆ ◆ ◆

Grandma's napkin, balled into a flower, flutters over the railing of the balcony. Grandma struggles to her feet, stretching out long fingers cramped by arthritis. Dad lets Aunt Sue calm her down. Grandma's confusion unsettles him, but she's never been the kind to put her own affection into words, and so neither does he.

At Grandpa's burial, Dad hunched his shoulders against the wind that blew his jacket into a bell. "When my grandfather died"—he struggled to read his notes—"I remember Dad saying at the funeral: *He was an honorable man, and people loved him*. . . . And this is what I'll say now, about him, although I can't help wondering where all that time has gone. . ."

I cannot remember my father speaking in public before then, or after. I was only ten at the time. But it occurred to me that one day I would be saying the same things about him.

◆ ◆ ◆

The next day is the hottest of the summer. Water steams off the ocean, and even the birds are tired; they call as if far away. After breakfast Aunt Sue and I bring Grandma down to sit by the water. Aunt Sue arranges her in a plastic folding chair and ties a white hat onto her head. Grandma takes out her sewing but leaves it on her lap without looking at it. She is watching the surf, which whitens on the shore like frost on the edge of a window.

"What are you working on, Gram?" I ask.

She turns to me and smiles. "Oh, a picture," she says. "It's a country house."

The picture is a flower, not a house. I'm not sure what the appropriate response is, so I tell her, "I liked the house you and Grandpa used to have up in Cooperstown. Courtney and I used to play in the attic when we were little."

"Oh, very nice," she says, nodding. I wonder if she even knows who I am.

"Are you okay like this in the sun? Do you want me to go find an umbrella?"

Suddenly, her smile drops away. She stares at me, horrified, and reaches for my arm.

"Gram? What's wrong?" I look to Aunt Sue for help, but she is engrossed in a book and does not seem to notice.

Just then Dad comes up behind us, a chair slung over his shoulder. Grandma hears him and twists around, her face lit up, as if nothing has happened. "Vern! Did you bring me my snacks?" She reaches for his bag.

Dad hands her a box of Poppycock, and Aunt Sue looks up and shakes her head. She puts a hand on Grandma's shoulder. "Hold on, Ma," she says. "Don't eat too much at once, you'll get sick."

Dad tries to unfold his chair; he has to tinker with it before he is able to pull it into shape. I want to help him, but I know it will only embarrass him. He always looks out of place on the beach. He doesn't own a bathing suit, and his legs are white as paper. He wears his sneakers with the socks pulled five inches above his ankles.

"Dad," I say. "Are we going to look at the cars tomorrow?"

"Sure," he says, as if were *my* idea.

I never want to, but I go because it is his favorite part of the summer. Every year we drive to Atlantic City to see the classic car show, and every summer he talks about buying one but never does. I think he's afraid not to have something to look forward to. When I left for college three years ago, it was difficult. Neither of us had ever been alone before. He was always a shy man who listened more than he spoke, and didn't like talking on the phone. He asked if he could write me letters, and I said okay, and when they arrived—elaborate notes handwritten on old, tissue-thin typing paper—I began to love him in a new way. When I was young, I loved him blindly, as a child will love her father. But when I grew older it became a different, truer kind of love, a love that sees everything.

By the time Courtney carries Ellie down from the house and everyone is on the beach, we have formed a little half-circle facing the water. Still, I can't think of a moment that felt lonelier. This time last year, there were ten of us, and the year before that, thirteen. Every summer another one of Dad's five siblings calls with an excuse—a work emergency, a child with hives. *Of course, next year,* they say; but Dad and I know better.

This year Uncle Carl, Aunt Sue's husband, is among those missing. He stayed home, I know, for the same reason as all the others— Grandma is too sick to notice anymore, and the Jersey shore bores them. When she moved into the senior care center and Sue and Carl took over her finances, they discovered that she had given away almost all of their inheritance since Grandpa died—tens of thousands of dollars a year to small, unrelated charities, groups she was never even a part of: the Detroit Zoological Society; the Portuguese American Citizen Forum—as if she had just opened her checkbook and chosen names at random.

I'm not sure why Dad insists on coming back every year. What does he owe her? I tell him he should use his vacation time to go to Italy, or Hawaii. But I know he won't. Partly, I know, summers in Ocean City remind him of Grandpa. But mostly, I think, he has nowhere else to go. He does not like to travel; he has never been out of New Jersey for more than two days except when he was in college.

✦ ✦ ✦

After only twenty minutes on the beach, the sun is bright as metal, and any trace of a breeze has disappeared. Courtney sighs and says she better take the baby back to the house before it gets too hot. She throws her bag over one shoulder and presses the baby to the other.

When she is far enough away, Dad asks Aunt Sue about Courtney's husband.

"Oh, he's fine," Sue says. "He's in Baghdad, I guess. Courtney doesn't like to talk about him, you know." She smiles, and it occurs to me that she and Courtney don't seem to talk very much at all. "Of course she's just worried about him," Aunt Sue adds quickly, "which is normal."

Grandma squirms in her chair. "I think I'd like to go back to the house now too," she says.

Aunt Sue closes her eyes. "We just got here, Ma."

"I know, but I want to go back. I'm hot."

"I'll take her," Dad offers, hoisting himself off the chair with one hand on his back. I think of him in the earlier years, jumping the waves with my small body on his shoulders.

I wave him back down. "No, Dad, I'll do it. I've been here longer anyway."

"Are you sure?"

I nod. "I don't mind. Do you want me to bring back Mack 'n' Manco's for lunch?"

"Yeah," he says, sinking back into his chair. "Get a pepperoni pie, would you? I'll call for it if you'll pick it up." He takes a $20 bill from his wallet.

I hold onto Grandma's forearm as we make our way through the sand toward the boardwalk. She waddles, clasping my shirt with one hand and her hat, still tied under her chin, with the other.

Off the coast in the distance, we can see Atlantic City. It is just a small cluster of buildings, misted by clouds, but at night it will be as bright as Manhattan.

I point to it. "Look, Gram, do you see Atlantic City over there?"

"What? Oh, yes," she says. "Good, good."

She is tired when we reach the boardwalk. She asks me to stop and rest on one of the benches. The benches are gray-blue, like the sea, spread fifty feet apart down the length of the boardwalk; their donors are identified with square bronze plaques. The bench we are sitting on has been purchased in loving memory of Daniel and Elaine, by their son, and Grandma runs her fingers over the indentation of the letters.

She turns to me again and takes my hand in hers. "I think, Angie," she says, looking out at the ocean, "Grandpa and I would like to have one of these benches someday."

"Who's Angie, Gram? I'm Erin. Don't you remember?"

"What?" Her eyes begin to tear.

"It's okay, Gram. We'll put your names on, okay?"

She leans back again, relieved, and pats my hand. "Tell them to put your name on it too."

"Thank you, Grandma, but I think it's better if it's just the two of you. It wouldn't be right for my name to be there."

"Don't be silly!" she says. She looks down at her hand. "It was a beautiful ring," she says wistfully. "Grandpa gave it to me. I lost it in the ocean the summer after we were married. What a fool I was . . ."

I imagine Grandma's engagement ring is still buried somewhere in the copper sand beneath the water. I imagine she believes she will find it one day, and this is why we kept coming back after Grandpa died.

"Let's go now, Ange," she says. "Help me stand up now."

I wonder if Angie is the name of the girl who fell. They say that some people, when they are very old, dream about things moving through the sky because they are thinking of angels.

* * *

When we arrive at the house, Courtney is curled up on the couch with a novel and a bowl of pink ice cream. She puts her finger to her mouth. "Ellie's asleep." She lifts the shade on the living room window and the light pours onto the floor like paint. Grandma wanders toward the bedroom.

"Are you taking a nap, Gram?"

She nods and rubs the skin of her cheeks up and down. "I'm so tired."

"Okay," I say. "You go in, and I'll get you some water."

I go back to the living room. In the kitchen, Courtney is hunched over the dining table. When I come closer, I see her hand deep inside Grandma's purse.

"What are you doing?"

She turns around quickly, slipping a roll of bills into her pocket. "Hey, Erin," she says brightly. "I thought I'd run down to Brown's and get Grandma some lunch. Do you want something?"

"I'm already getting pizza. My dad's ordering it. Grandma said she wanted some."

"Oh." She hesitates, but doesn't retrieve the money from her pocket.

"Come on," I say. "You were taking the money for yourself."

"I was not!" She glares at me.

"Well, why don't you put it back, then?"

"Shhhh." She waves at me to lower my voice. "Ellie's *sleeping*. Just leave it alone, Erin. It's only $30."

Leave it alone? I think. How am I supposed to leave it alone? "What if she needs that money?" I counter. "You know she's got almost nothing left, don't you? Your mom's the one who's gonna have to pay for her room if she runs out!"

Courtney laughs. "*My* mom? What about your dad? He doesn't do a thing for her. My mom and I, we're the ones who've been looking after her for years! *Your* dad should pay for her!"

"Don't talk about my dad that way," I say, my fists clenched. "You know he barely makes enough to help me with college. Besides, you *like* to take care of her. You *like* being the *good* granddaughter, because you get attention for it, and then you think it gives you the right to reward yourself with Grandma's things."

Courtney shakes her head. "Listen, Erin. You've got it all wrong. Grandma *tells* me to take from her. All my life, she's told me that what's hers is mine too. I'm not doing anything wrong. And I *need* this money. Bill barely makes anything."

"Seriously, I know you're not *poor*, okay? Your parents have money."

"Do you think they'd give me anything?" She laughs and shakes her head. "They hate Bill. When I got married, I was on my own."

"But you get *everything* else." Still aware of Ellie, I am whispering, but so loudly my voice is hoarse. "Grandma *loves* you. She paid for your wedding dress, your car, your tuition . . ."

"I didn't ask for any of that," she says, holding up her hands.

"But you took it! My dad and I don't get anything like that. We don't take from her. And she doesn't even know who I am! She's calling me other names." I turn away. "It's not fair to me. It's like—having a mother favor one child over another, right out in the open."

Courtney shakes her head. "She's not your mother, though."

"I know that!"

"You can't take what she does seriously. I'm not talking about just now. Even before she was sick. She hasn't had the best life."

I laugh. "Grandpa gave her everything she wanted. She never had to work. All those dresses, the jewelry, the parties. . ."

Courtney shrugs. "Well, her life wasn't perfect," she says. "No one's is. And besides, you know she started giving me those things as a baby because she was upset about my sister dying. It's got nothing to do with me."

Her admission startles me. There is such deep sadness in it. I realize, for the first time, that Courtney isn't getting Grandma's love; she's getting what was meant for her dead sister. And Courtney knows it.

I decide to let the $30 go, because I'm sure it's what my dad would do. And because for a moment, in my forgiving her, it feels like we are children again—friends and not rivals—and the beaches are noisy with life, and we are paddling in the sea with our ears plugged, apart from all the problems of the world.

I remember the way she cried when she found out she was pregnant, because Bill was drunk in some bar, bloated and glassy-eyed, on his way to Iraq a week later. We were in this same house. She cried in front of Dad and me, and Aunt Sue, instead of comforting her, pulled her into the bathroom, mortified. When they emerged Courtney's face was solemn and dry, her cheeks newly bronzed.

Ellie's shriek rises from the other room. Courtney rushes to the baby's bedroom, clutching a paper towel to her face, leaving me alone in the middle of the kitchen, the fluorescent lights softened by the sun.

◆ ◆ ◆

When I bring the pizza back down to the beach, I see Dad sitting alone by the water. The pink faces of shells look up from the sand like jewels, but I have walked this way enough times to know that when I kick them over, their undersides are ugly and brown.

"Where's Aunt Sue?" I ask, trying to sound casual, reclining into the chair next to him.

"Uncle Carl called. She went off somewhere with her cell phone."

I nod, laying the pizza box on the sand.

"How's Grandma?" Dad opens the box. The smells bring the seagulls from their perches.

I hand him a napkin. "Fine. She's sleeping. She wants a bench, though. One of those on the boardwalk. In hers and Grandpa's names."

Dad laughs. "I'm sure she does."

"What do you mean?" I ask, surprised. I've never heard him talk about her so bitterly.

"She wants a lot of things."

When we were younger Courtney and I searched Grandma and Grandpa's basement in Cooperstown. Behind the *National Geographic*s we found boxes of letters Dad had written when he was my age, in college at Penn State. "I hate it here," he wrote. "If I don't get picked up for the draft I want to transfer." The words were flung blue-inked across the page, like bruises. It had occurred to me that one day I would be older than he was when he wrote those letters.

But he never transferred; his diploma hangs on the wall in his office. I imagine it had something to do with Grandma and her unwavering sense of propriety. Like Sue and Courtney, she does not admit to unhappiness. It is a defense my father learned from her.

"Dad," I say suddenly. "Who's Angie?"

He looks at me sharply. "Angie? Why?"

"Grandma called me Angie."

"Oh." He doesn't respond apart from this. Beyond him, the sea heaves as the wind picks up.

"Dad?"

"Angie was Courtney's sister," he says.

"The one who died? No—her name was Emily."

"Grandma always called her by her middle name, Angie."

"Why didn't I know that?"

Dad shakes his head. "You never asked," he says, and I realize he is right. I can't even remember how, exactly, she died.

I grope for some excuse. "Still, you could have told me. . ."

"When was I supposed to tell you? When you were little, I didn't want you going around asking hurtful questions because you didn't know any better. Then you got older, and I thought, what would be the point of bringing it up again, after all this time?"

He moves the sand around with his toes. "Grandma was watching her when Aunt Sue was in the hospital having Courtney. Grandma woke up and the baby had died." He sighs. "It wasn't her fault. There was no way to know what would happen."

"But why would she call *me* Angie?"

He shrugs. "Who knows? Probably because you were the next grandchild to be born after Courtney. Even after all that time, Grandma wouldn't come near you for years."

"She was afraid of me?" I test out the words. It sounds crazy when I say it out loud. "But—all those things she gave to Courtney. You let me think I didn't get them because she didn't care!"

Dad laughs. "She offered you lots of things, Erin, for years. Toys, books, clothes. I thought you knew that."

I look at him doubtfully. "I don't remember anything like that."

"Well," he says, holding up his hands, "when you were about seven or so, I told her to stop. So I guess it's my fault, really. That's what she does, you see. She gives things. That's what she always did with me. I didn't want you growing up like that."

He sounds so resentful. I wonder who made him that way more, Grandma or my mother.

"Dad," I say. "You don't *hate* Grandma, though, do you?"

"No," he says and chews his lip. "But I don't know if I love her either."

I can't believe he is saying these things. It's not like him at all. He's such a gentle man. But what can I say—*She's an old woman?* It is a silly excuse, but for some reason it seems to matter.

Still, I think, she must have been loving once. She loved my grandfather, after all. Or maybe it was my grandfather who loved her. Either way, I know what Dad's thinking, that it won't matter much longer. This may be our last year. Next year everything might be different. It will be just the two of us again, Dad and me. I think he will be happy when that is the case. I think we will both be relieved.

I want to say more, about what happened with Courtney, about how I wonder if Courtney's husband is messing around. When people like Bill, like my mother, get tied down, they want to leave, and then one day they do.

Aunt Sue returns from her phone conversation and rushes to gather her things. She points to the sky. "Black clouds," she says. "Let's go."

"We'll be up in a minute," Dad says. "You go on ahead."

"All right, but you'll get soaked!" she warns as she hurries away.

I wait for Dad. The sky purples with rain. After a few minutes he stands up, and we walk back together, slowly. We don't talk, but I know we have come to some kind of understanding, that we are alone in this family together.

In the house we find Courtney sitting at the dining room table, cradling Ellie against her shoulder. "Grandma can't remember my name anymore," she says flatly. "All of a sudden. I never thought it would get to that point."

Her hair is still perfectly tied up. She sits like a ballerina.

"She's asking about Grandpa now. She thinks he's down at the beach. What am I supposed to say to that?"

Whether or not we have really forgiven each other, I know we will never discuss what happened between us. In our family, we don't talk about those kinds of things.

The baby fusses in her arms. I wonder if Ellie will begin talking soon, whether she learns something new every time Grandma forgets. I imagine that the parts of Grandma that are leaving, ever so slowly, pass into Ellie on their way out.

Three days later, our week at the house expires. Dad and I strap our bicycles onto the back of his car. I will stay home with him for a month until the semester begins. Dad and I get into one car, and Grandma, Aunt Sue, and Courtney get into another. We all open our windows so we can smell the salt air as we drive away.

Dad lets Aunt Sue back out of the driveway first. As she turns onto the street, I wave. "Bye, Gram!" I call out the window. It is a difficult thing to say. Grandma leans out of the car as far as she can, but she is not looking at me. She is looking for the ocean or for Grandpa; I'm not sure which. As we watch them go, I turn and see Dad studying my face, his head cocked to the side. He reaches out and pushes a strand of hair behind my ear.

"There," he says.

Acknowledgments

The following stories have been published previously:

"Finding the Good Light" in *Carolina Quarterly*

"Prayers of an American Wife" in *Southwest Review*

"The Strangers of Dubai" in *South Carolina Review*

"The Whispering Gallery" in *Owen Wister Review*

"All the Ways We Say Goodbye" in *Colorado Review*

"A Home Like Someone Else's Home" in *Alaska Quarterly Review*

"Tonight Everything Will Be Quiet and Still" in *Great River Review*

"Waiting for the Creel" in *Fiction*

"The Chimney" in *Greensboro Review*

"The Wedding" in *Idaho Review*

"Rachel's Story" in *Freight Stories*

"What Happened on Crystal Mountain" in *Scrivener Creative Review*

"Little Angels, Little Dolls" in *Slice Magazine*

About the Author

VICTORIA KELLY is the author of the novel *Mrs. Houdini* and the poetry collections *When the Men Go Off to War* and *Prayers of an American Wife*. Her fiction and poetry have appeared in *Best American Poetry, The Autumn House Anthology of Contemporary American Poetry, Prairie Schooner, Alaska Quarterly Review, Southwest Review,* and numerous other journals. She graduated from Harvard University and received master's degrees from the Iowa Writers' Workshop and Trinity College Dublin, where she was a US Mitchell Scholar.